TURQUOISE TRAVELLER

Also by David John Griffin

The Unusual Possession of Alastair Stubb (2015)
Infinite Rooms (2016)
Two Dogs At The One Dog Inn And Other Stories (2017)
Abbie and the Portal (2018)

TURQUOISE
TRAVELLER

DAVID JOHN GRIFFIN

Dedicated to my loyal readers

"The imagination is a palette of bright colors. You can use it to touch up memories — or you can use it to paint dreams."

Robert Brault

"Who in the world am I? Ah, that's the great puzzle."

Lewis Carroll, *Alice in Wonderland*

"But what really matters is not what you believe but the faith and conviction with which you believe…"

Knut Hamsun, *Mysteries*

"Your head has dissolved into thin air and I can see the rhododendrons through your stomach. It's not that you are dead or anything dramatic like that, it is simply that you are fading away and I can't even remember your name."

Leonora Carrington, *The Hearing Trumpet*

"Deep into that darkness peering, long I stood there, wondering, fearing, doubting, dreaming dreams no mortal ever dared to dream before."

Edgar Allan Poe, *The Raven*

CHAPTERS

1 : REVOLVING THE DARK

STAVE SWIRLER SAT on a double-decker bus that travelled in the blackest of nights. He knew something significant had occurred at the moment he held up cough mixture to a strip light. Prismatic shapes swam within the bottle. Chimes and the odour of menthol subtly emanated from its dark brown glass.

Peculiar.

That was a benign signal for him to replace the cough mixture into a pocket of his turquoise jacket.

He shuffled a hand in a plastic bag beside him to extract an apple. An odd saying flashed through his muffled mind.

An apple a day keeps the monsters away.

The precise moment his teeth entered the flesh of the crisp fruit, a quiet voice from behind said, 'I adore oranges.' And with a roar of the engine, the double-decker bus left the outside world and entered a tunnel.

Leaving night-time, the known darkness. Swallowed.

Sodium-vapour lamps instantly replaced with similar within that tunnel burrowed by vast multi-toothed machines under the slow river.

Drafts of foul-smelling air rushed through the bus from

an unknown source.

What a stench. Like rotting food.

The smell clung in his throat and nose, his eyes watering. Stave considered drinking some of his cough mixture when the thought occurred to him that he was not aware of having a cough. But then the air cleared and he decided there was no need for cough mixture either way.

No past thoughts. My mind feeling strange with memories erased. Or blocked. Washed with black ink. That's the only way to describe it. What am I doing on this bus? Can't remember where I'm going or where I've been. A nagging sense that reality has altered in a significant way.

Now a quiet bus engine – more of a modulated hum – as it passed ribs of concrete within the long tunnel. A cluster of lamps, a forty miles per hour sign, a telephone stuck to the wall like a large wart, an air-conditioning fan, then another concrete rib. Almost hypnotic in its repetition. Pulsing light with a pulsing sound of thick air, throbbing as the bus engine pulsed as well, in hummed rhythm.

Then the hum resonated like a hive of wasps in an echo chamber, making wax in Stave Swirler's ears pop.

Something's not right. I have a strong feeling of an unusual occurrence, a premonition that badness is going to happen. Maybe the engine is going to stall in this tunnel. And such a long tunnel, almost as if it's never-ending. Deeply worrying.

The absence of natural light, absence of understanding, absence of memory.

Panic rose in his throat, making him quake. He wondered if he was coming down with a fever. He held a palm to his forehead but didn't feel overly hot. He thought to undo his turquoise tie from about his neck or loosen the collar of his white shirt but changed his mind.

Nagging feelings of worry were still with him. Another bite to the apple calmed him – he no longer shivered.

He saw a neat hole inside the apple, the size of a nail head, though there wasn't a hole outside on the red-to-green skin. Perhaps he had eaten the entry point of the grub, beetle or wasp; or whatever other tiny, burrowing organism it had been. At the bottom of the hole, near the core and the pips, was a small object catching the bus's fluorescent light. Stave dug a finger into the fruit and clawed at the apple flesh with a fingernail, then extracted the item with a finger and thumb. It was a tiny feather, made of ochre-coloured metal. It had fine details on its quill and vanes, yet was no more than four centimetres in length.

Interesting, I'll keep that. Amazing what can be found inside apples.

He carefully placed the find in the right-hand pocket of his turquoise trousers.

A flash within his thoughts – the word "adventure" jolting into his mind, then it was gone.

His attention was caught by the advertisements along the top of the bus windows. They showed flashing smiles from vacant models, and images of products held up, with slogans such as, "Buy two, get the third twice the price!" and "Go here instead of there – you know it makes sense".

Stave creased his brow at the preposterous statements.

Loud expressions of someone else's absurd mind.

He ate more of the apple, but the skin and flesh of it had become bitter. He carefully wrapped the half-eaten fruit in a striped handkerchief taken from a waistcoat pocket and placed it back into the plastic bag. He brushed his suit trousers with the edge of a palm before adjusting his tie.

What signals the beginning of a descent into a type of madness? No prescience, a wiping away of any warning…

With a howling roar like the cry of a massive, prehistoric beast, the whole of the road tunnel, with flat floor and ceiling, and curved sides, began quickly rotating anti-clockwise. It took a while to register in Stave's brain as to what was happening. Then he realised the impossible was occurring. He fastened his seat belt.

This is serious, we are going to crash; we're sure to die.

The bottom of the bus scraped along the left walkway with screeching and a shower of bright sparks, then was travelling along the left wall that had become the ground. The bus swerved to avoid hitting the obstacles – the grills, telephones and speed signs – bumping over the tunnel's concrete ribs. Stave gripped the seat rail in front of him, bouncing up and down while the quivering bus was thrown violently about.

It's a wonder the side mirror hasn't been smashed off. A surprise I haven't been knocked out.

The bus was steadied, being driven at an angle in the opposite way of the tunnel spinning, to keep it upright. The driver was performing an admirable job under the peculiar circumstances.

'It's OK, nothing to worry about,' came a sturdy voice from the driver's compartment of the bus. The vehicle was now being driven along what had been the ceiling of the tunnel, the metal-encased lights clanking against the underside of it. 'I do believe we're still the right way around.'

Whichever that was, or is. This doesn't normally happen, I'm certain. Feeling giddy and unnatural.

'What is the right way around?' Stave questioned out loud, more to himself than anyone else. But he felt embarrassed at vocalising such an obvious question.

The driver in his cabin heard and answered back via the intercom. His voice, crackling with static, came from speakers along the length of the bus.

'Ask someone the opposite side of the world,' he said and chuckled dryly. 'What is up, what is down? What's sideways, for that matter. Bleating haven, bleeding blade – hang on to your hats.'

Now the whole of the tunnel had revolved even more, so that the right-hand wall had become the ground. And after the bus had flattened the railings there, the tyres finally found the real floor again. With sounds of metal being twisted and shearing, the mighty tunnel stopped rotating.

The bus continued, uninterrupted.

'Everyone still in one piece?' the driver continued in a loud voice, this time without the use of the intercom, his words dulled by the driver's cabin. 'I often dream this, no apology needed. I'm a good character. I live in the best part of the city near the park, and I'll be meeting my destiny today. That's all I can recall at the moment. Enough now, I must concentrate on the driving.'

Stave had been holding his seat so tightly, his knuckles and fingers had turned white. He relaxed.

So, I'm in someone else's dream. Interesting. Totally ludicrous, though. For a dream, it's very real. But then for reality, it's most dreamlike.

Still the pulsing of sound and vision, still the concrete ribs, the lights, telephones and railings, passing time after time.

If this were my dream, I'd have the tunnel slither away, the river dry, to leave a delightful village setting to explore on the ancient riverbed. Hmm, strange thinking on my part.

Stave studied the murky glass panes, each one large enough to afford vision of the ghostly reflection of the seats in the bus. The yellow light from the tunnel lamps turned to a dimmed orange.

With the suddenly reduced lighting of the tunnel and the bright strip lights within, the interior became more prominent in the reflections. Stave couldn't see the driver in his cabin seat controlling the vehicle but could easily see the other travellers by turning his head to the left to look behind him at their reflections.

On the opposite side of the bus, further down, there were two other passengers. Four people, including the bus driver, travelling through the tunnel.

Not a busy bus service.

On the penultimate seat before the back sat one of those passengers, a young man with shaved sides to his head. Not much younger than himself, Stave considered. A welt of black hair covered his forehead. This was in contrast to Stave's full head of hair with his receding hairline. The young man wore a red costume eye mask, held over his eyes with an elastic band. And he cradled a bottle of fine champagne in his arms, tapping fingers of one hand onto the glass. He had a studded dog collar around his neck.

Behind him on the back seat was a young woman with prominent features, deep-set and serious eyes, pale skin, and mahogany hair tied into a pigtail. She was attractive in her own way. She wore a flowing dress, printed with images of marbles. She was unwrapping newspaper parcels taken from a holdall beside her. The parcels contained wooden fish – carp, barbell, and tench amongst others – all of them carefully carved with precision. The scales, fins, and heads were beautifully rendered. She inspected each one carefully before wrapping it again in the newspaper and returning it to the holdall. She hummed a song, a pretty melody, contrasting with the hum of the bus engine. Even from where Stave was sitting he could smell her lavender perfume.

The same gravelly voice of the bus driver came over the intercom again.

'As you were. If we all get along, then there's no fear. That's one of my mottos I made up. Fear only makes you fear the more. Don't fear the feared – go with the flow. Next stop is when we get out of this crazy tunnel. At least, you might get off there. Who am I to say? I'm awaiting further instructions.'

The agitated voice of the young man was heard as he talked with urgency to the lady with the wooden fish.

'Did the tunnel turn or did we? I've a good mind to report this to the authorities. Though all has calmed down now so I'll try to forget it. You alright? You look placid enough.'

Whatever answer the young man received didn't reach Stave's ears and all he heard was the sound of static, as if coming from a badly tuned radio.

The engine throbbed again, the pulse almost keeping pace with Stave's heartbeats. He became restless, bringing to mind that he had forgotten why he was on the bus or even what his destination might be.

The tunnel was relentless. Already they had been travelling through it for five minutes.

It must be a wide river we are under or maybe it's a mountain we're going through.

He inspected his ticket taken from his turquoise trousers pocket. Perhaps that would give some indication of his destination. He unfolded it. The back of the ticket bore the bus company's logo consisting of a circle with a spot in the middle, and four green arrows pointing to it. The ink was faint on the front side, the only clear type being a ten-digit number and the words, "Price: you pay" in red lettering.

More ludicrous nonsense.

By impulse, Stave looked up and raised an eyebrow. How had he not seen the coffee machine before, the one opposite the luggage area at the front of the bus?

It must be a progressive bus company. Such refreshment possibilities are usually found only on coaches.

The bus still travelled the steadied tunnel road, passing rib after rib of concrete. Between them, more advertisements in neon, and enamelled signs, advertised "Coffee in all its Glory", "Don't Race Past Pastry" and "Unidentified Tea, No Cups".

Stave stood. While steadying himself by holding onto the green rails along the bus aisle, he walked up to the black box that was the coffee machine. Between the machine and the driver's cabin was a staircase leading to the bus upper deck. Beside the machine were a cake dispenser, a cast iron kettle, and a microscope.

A strange place to have scientific equipment.

Steam squealed from the kettle spout, sounding like a

piglet trapped in quicksand in the distance. The coffee machine shook now and then as though alive and cold. He watched coffee drip from its spout into a plastic cup. A sign on the machine read, "You should know better".

While idly pressing the buttons on the cake dispenser marked "cakes", "more cakes" and "even more cakes", he fumbled in a pocket with the other hand for a coin. To his surprise, an item appeared in the plastic tray at the base of the dispenser with a clunking of its mechanism, without the need of payment. It was a grey cake with blue currants.

He took it, turning it over in his hand, with an irresistible desire to eat it. He bit into it with a fervent passion. The first mouthful was delicious. It had an indefinable flavour, unlike any other cake he had ever tasted.

That's good.

He took another bite. There was something hard inside. He extracted the object from his mouth. It looked like a lump of rock, possibly calcium carbonate from mollusc shells or teeth.

He placed the find, about the size of a small coin, onto a glass slide of the microscope. It seemed a natural thing to do on finding a piece of rock inside a free cake, to inspect it under a microscope that had been conveniently left there. He adjusted the focus wheel while peering through the top lens.

Filling his vision was a black prism, refracting white light into various shades of grey and blue. The greys were as disturbing as the sight of infected vegetables, or decaying vision in the midst of a migraine. The blues were like toxic fumes. They were difficult to keep his attention upon, a stroboscopic effect making him feel light-headed while examining them. As disturbing and dizzying as they were, there was a fascination that kept him looking through the lens. He tore his sight away only upon hearing the sharp ringing of metal on metal, coming from the upper floor of the bus.

2 : STRANGERS IN THE DREAM

STAVE CLIMBED THE rubber-coated stairs. On his ascent of the spiral staircase were more advertisements in plastic frames on one side, proclaiming, "Beware below as above" and "Beginning of the end".

He reached the top deck of the bus and looked to his right. Strangely, the driver was there in his cabin, driving. Upon looking opposite, he saw the luggage rack where the cast iron kettle now stood, along with the coffee machine, cake dispenser, and microscope.

There were blue shutters over the windows. At the back, where the young woman with her wooden fish sat directly below, was a goldfish out of its water, flopping and twitching on the patterned bus seat.

And there, in the aisle next to where Stave had been sitting below, stood the dramatic figure of a man dressed in black trousers and a leather apron. He was more than seven feet tall, his head touching the ceiling of the bus. He wielded a heavy mallet, striking a metal object with vigorous force. The object, in the shape of a diamond, was being flattened on a blackened anvil. His left foot pushed down on bellows. The bellows were giving oxygen to hot coals in a brown cardboard box. He looked up to meet Stave's gaze, then continued his work. His eyes were fiercely determined.

A harlequin, wearing a white, pointed hat and with a chalk white face with black lipstick, sat in the position directly above that of the young man on the floor below. There was a set of tongs in his slim hands. He waved the tongs in some prescribed pattern until, like a magician's trick, a lump of coal appeared in the grip of them. He flung the tongs over his shoulder, the coal flying from them to the back. It bounced off the rear window of the bus and flew forward towards the front, landing neatly into the cardboard box containing the burning coals.

He constantly repeated the ritualistic procedure: the waving of the tongs, the coal appearing, throwing the coal over the shoulder of his diamond-patterned costume – just missing his pointed hat – and then, from the rebound, the coal neatly landing into the box.

Why doesn't the box burn or catch alight?

Stave went to talk with the bus driver but now his seat was empty, the steering wheel turning slightly left and slightly right, adjusting the wheels along its path as if being driven by remote control.

'Careful of the dance,' the harlequin said with deep sorrow within his thin and high voice. Now his white face was smeared with soot.

'What dance?' Stave asked.

The harlequin spoke on with sadness still tainting his words.

'I used to be the most exalted mime artist in the world. I travelled to all parts of the globe – north, south, east, and west. I entertained so well, the audience would refuse to leave, and when finally releasing me from my performance would applaud continually for an hour. That was until the agents of Tremelon gave me a voice. But it was the wrong voice. Now I can speak, I no longer mime. Except the mime of the dangers of hot coals.'

'But that's no mime, I must mention. It's a conjuring trick. Real coals are appearing in the tongs you hold.'

'You see how weak my talents have become, so diluted as to be practically non-existent? I was under the impression I mimed holding tongs and the plucking of coals from the evil realm.'

'Tell me more about this realm, if you wouldn't mind,' Stave said.

A gust of wind from nowhere, words springing into Stave Swirler's mind: *a dream wind.* A howling of a storm from outside, making the bus rock and creak as it progressed along the tunnel.

I don't understand how there can be a storm in a tunnel. But then I didn't understand why the tunnel revolved…

The ironmonger interrupted Stave's train of thought.

'Get out while you can,' he said in a deep, baritone voice as he took metal cutters from the pocket of his leather apron.

'I would if I knew how. Are you in your own dream or someone else's?' Stave replied.

And if you are within my dream, why would I dream you?

'I am a member of the dream cast. But whose dream I used to be part of I've become unaware, and now no longer will I discover.'

'Both of you, part of the driver's dream perhaps?' Stave

asked, but he received no answer. 'Or maybe even from one of the two passengers downstairs?'

The ironmonger scooped up a handful of the hot coals and held them out to Stave. He smelled the odour of charcoal and ash, and burning flesh.

'Better than what is to come,' the tall blacksmith said.

'What do you mean?'

'I mean that whoever's dream it was, it's no longer. It has been taken over and we have become a part of Tremelon Zandar's dream.'

Stave shuddered as if cold fingers scratched his back. He hadn't known the name and yet, at the same time, it seemed so familiar once it had been spoken. Anxiety gripped him as he sensed the unreal situation. The dream wind in the bus vanished and he was hot, feeling intense heat coming from the burning coals in the cardboard box. The storm still raged outside.

'I'm out of here,' he replied and clattered back down the stairs of the moving bus.

He heard the ironmonger call out as he went, along with another ringing of metal upon metal, 'You can't get out, at least not at the beginning.'

That man talks in riddles.

As Stave descended, he attempted to slow his fast beating heart; he must calm down to assess the peculiar situation he found himself in.

When he had reached the ground floor, the storm outside had ceased. He saw the driver at the wheel again, and the youth and young woman sitting in their seats, both quiet and content within their own thoughts.

3 : FORGETFULNESS AND GREETINGS

As STAVE WALKED down the length of the bus towards the other two passengers, he heard the words, 'What's your destination?'

Stave reached his seat, sat with his legs in the aisle, and replied to the young man wearing the costume eye mask, 'I'm going to – to...'

How could I forget where I'm going? And now I think about it, I've no recollection of my life, how old I am, if I've a family. But why? Too much wine with friends, not enough fresh air or sunshine, not enough sleep? A blow to the head even? Whatever the reason for sudden forgetfulness, it's deeply worrying. Perhaps I'm sick with an insidious, subtle fever, after all. That could account for talking with a depressed harlequin and a weird ironmonger.

He stood, a quick decision entering his mind to find out his journey's end. Holding on to the backs of the seats, he made his way to the front of the bus, where he held onto a yellow handle by the pneumatic doors, opposite the stairs.

'Where is this bus going?' he asked the bus driver.

The driver stared implacably ahead as if hypnotised from the regular rhythm of the lights and concrete ribs, as they

15

passed on the curved walls of the tunnel.

'Can't talk, I'm driving. Not allowed to talk. But I'm enjoying the drive, tell you that much. Great fun. I've always wanted to be a bus driver ever since I was a nipper. Even in a dream. If I'm dreaming you, then I'll eventually let you know.'

'All you have to do is tell me the destination, now. Are we going to the cinema? To a sports stadium or a race track?'

There was a pause.

'The bus goes forwards,' the driver suddenly replied, 'and sometimes backwards. Even tries to rotate, as we've all discovered.'

'Are you trying to be funny?' Without being given a reply, Stave shook his head and gave a tut. 'I've a good mind to report you,' he muttered. On the way back to his seat, he called out to the youth, 'Can you tell me where we're going? It's silly, I know, but it seems I have developed a form of amnesia.'

The young woman on the back seat looked up but then resumed studying one of her fish, inspecting the carved gills and sniffing its wooden fragrance.

The youth spoke while fingering his studded dog collar.

'Were you hoping to spend money, see some sights, or watch a band, or a game? My guess is, with your sharp turquoise suit, white shirt, and stylish tie, you are off for an interview.'

'I'm not sure. Spend money, possibly. Going shopping perhaps, though I don't think so.'

The young man nodded, now adjusting the eye mask by its elastic band.

16

'If you are, then you're going to a shopping mall, possibly on the outskirts of a city.' He pointed to one of the advertisements above a window of the bus. The image showed an anonymous tower block, the words, "The Shopping Mall, on the outskirts of the city" printed across it. 'You're smartly dressed to go shopping in your neat suit. What are you going to buy? Food, more clothes, a mobile, plants, crockery? A pet? A dog, cat, ferret, lizard, maybe? A lizard would be cool.'

'None of those things, as far as I'm aware,' Stave answered. 'Maybe I'm going to a restaurant.'

'With a lizard?' asked the young man with a serious tilt of the head.

The surreal conversation gripped him with a dream-like force.

Stave was about to answer, when his attention was drawn again to the young woman on the back seat, now gazing at one of the larger fish from her holdall. This one had been skilfully and delicately painted in bright colours.

'I wouldn't take a lizard to a restaurant,' the young man continued. 'Not even to the gathering.'

Stave met his eyes again.

'That's where you are going, is it, a gathering?'

The young man didn't answer for a few seconds.

'I admit, I can't completely remember either.'

'The bus driver says he's dreaming,' Stave said. 'Do you believe you are in his dream?'

'Now you mention dreams – I'm hoping to meet a dream instructor at the gathering, that much I can recall now.'

'I wonder what a dream instructor is,' Stave said.

'I've no idea,' the young man replied. 'Back to talking about the driver, I heard him say that too, that we were in his dream, when he pinned this rosette on me.'

He pointed to a dark blue-centred rosette with eight grey ribbons around it, attached to the lapel of his black leather jacket.

Why Stave hadn't noticed it before he couldn't be certain.

'When did he do that? Haven't seen him walk down the bus.'

'When we were in the previous tunnel, after the bus ran out of fuel.'

'There was a previous tunnel?'

'Yes, identical to this one,' the young man said. 'And after someone from the bus garage came along in his white van and filled it with petrol, we set off again. We carried on along the tunnel, out onto a short piece of dark road, then back into this tunnel. That's when you appeared. From nowhere. You weren't there in the first tunnel but then you were – here you are – in the second one, even though the bus didn't stop.'

'Forgetting stuff or not, that doesn't make sense.'

'Nor to me.'

'Let's get this right,' Stave said. 'Identical tunnel before this one and the bus broke down—'

'Ran out of—'

'Ran out of petrol and the bus driver pinned the rosette onto you. Why?'

'I haven't the faintest idea. I tried to unpin it but I can't. Don't know how the bus driver fastened it.'

'I'll try for you, if you like.'

'OK, cheers,' said the young man, as Stave stood and went

over to him, bending to take hold of the rosette.

He immediately let go with a howl.

'What the…my fingers are burnt. Are you playing some practical joke on me?'

'No, really I'm not. Sorry, I would never have meant to do that,' replied the young man with his palms facing Stave. 'That is bizarre – show me your hand.' Stave's fingertips were bright red and hot. 'Mine went so cold, I shivered so much I couldn't feel the pin. It was as if I had frostbite.'

Stave licked the ends of his sore fingers.

'I believe you,' he said, though suspicious and undecided whether he did or not.

The young man continued, 'Anyway, do you really think you are in his dream, appearing from nowhere the way you did? I have my own dreams, thank you, and this could be one of them, I'm guessing. So you and the driver, and the lady behind me, are in my dream, I've decided. But haven't we had this conversation before?'

Stave ignored the question to ask, 'Do you feel like you're dreaming?'

'Yes and no. Either it's a very real dream or an unreal reality.'

'That's what I thought. But still, I'm as real as you.'

'How can I believe that?' the young man replied.

'How can I believe you saying, "how can I believe that"? If this is anyone's dream then it's mine,' Stave answered with slight annoyance. 'Yet it's all so real for me, most of the time. Maybe you're in my dream and I'm in yours. But how can that be? Punch me.'

'Pardon?'

'Hit me. I want to see if I can feel it.'

The young man shrugged and did as Stave had requested. 'Well?' he said.

'Yes, I felt that, alright,' Stave replied, massaging the muscle at the top of his right arm. 'So this a real dream in reality, that's my guess.'

'Whatever that means. I had a real dream once when the sunrise was the colours of bruised fruit, and I was pushing a horse up the stairs leading to that damaged sky. It wouldn't budge. Stubborn animal. The harder I pushed, the more it resisted and the more it resisted, the more I pushed. Totally ludicrous, yet, at the time, it seemed real. Another one: I saw a pointed flint in the back garden. I attempted to dig it out but the further down I dug, the larger and wider it got. I decided I must bury the flint again but it was too fast for me. It continued to grow upwards at a faster rate than I could cover it until it was the size of a small mountain. I climbed it, right to the top. A long way, but didn't take me long in the dream.'

'And then?'

'At the summit, I looked around. I was balancing on a flint in my back garden. That was so realistic, I actually went out to the garden the next day, to see if I could find it.'

'That's strange and funny at the same time,' Stave said. 'I can't even remember my dreams, let alone anything else. And all of this talk about dreams is making my head spin. Now you mention a garden though, I suddenly remember I live in a cottage somewhere. At least, I think I do. And I'm on a bus going somewhere else. That's it. Apart from my name, that is. I remember that. Stave Swirler, by the way. And your name?'

'Quikso Lebum,' the young man replied. 'Pleased to meet you,' and he shook Stave's hand.

Stave turned to the young woman sitting on the back seat. 'And you are, may I ask?'

She looked up from inspecting her wooden fish.

'I am what? I don't rightly know. If you want to hear about my recurring nightmare, it involves pins, lots of them. No needles, just pins. And trapped in a lighthouse with other lighthouses advancing upon me. They are massive and about to swallow me whole. That's all I'm saying. And if you mean what is my name, I'm not sure it's any of your business.'

Her expressionless face became as yellow as a fresh banana skin.

'He was only being friendly,' Quikso Lebum said. 'And you appear to have turned a bright yellow.'

'You'll turn orange again if you're not careful. I saw it happen earlier. I'm in no mood to be friendly, as it happens,' she replied. 'I was promised dream tunnels and that's all I know. I can't even remember what a dream tunnel is. But if you are that desperate to know my name, as it seems, it's Mariella. Mariella Fortana.'

'Stave Swirler, pleased to meet you too.'

An ice cream van had appeared in the other lane of the tunnel and while matching speed, it travelled beside the bus. A crazy jingle of a tune came from it. Stave moved across to the right side and looked out from one of the windows. For an unknown reason to him, he was startled and felt his chest, his heart pumping blood at twice the rate as normal.

'Hold on tight, everyone,' the bus driver said over the

intercom, 'I may have to avoid this van,' and the bus picked up speed.

'Excuse me for a moment,' Stave Swirler said to Mariella Fortana and Quikso Lebum and he walked the length of the bus over to the driver's compartment once more.

'Step back behind the line while the bus is moving,' the driver stated.

'But I need to know why you're trying to avoid an ice cream van,' Stave said.

'Do you know nothing? Do you want my dream to turn into a good nightmare or a bad one? Haven't you heard of the agents of Tremelon? Do you believe they are evil or just misunderstood? I'm still uncertain. I've heard good things and bad things. Islands drowning in the ocean. Or uplifted spheres of positive evil. Now will you let me concentrate? Have you any idea concerning the nature of your own existence?'

'I don't know what you're talking about. What on earth does that last question even mean? You are very much a confusing person.'

'We'll all be most confused and more if we don't move away from that van soon. I'm not ready to meet an agent. I haven't made up my mind,' the bus driver replied as he scratched his scalp under his cap. 'What's he up to now, that van driver? I can't see in my side mirror now, after I caught him with his head in my direction.'

'I'll find out for you,' Stave said, and he walked back down the aisle of the bus.

The kettle next to the coffee machine, both opposite the luggage compartment, let out squeals, and a string of black and blue steam.

A roll top hatch was pulled upwards on the side of the ice cream van as it sped beside the rapidly moving bus.

'Slow down!' Stave called out to the driver, 'you can't beat it, no matter how fast you drive. You're putting us all in danger.'

The jingle from the van transformed into more squeals from the kettle, along with echoed cries, as if from voices of people trapped in a cave.

Stave watched with unexpected fascination as the large plastic ice cream cone on the van's roof rotated like a searching radar device. Then a grim figure appeared at the serving hatch at the side of the van.

4 : AN AGENT OF TREMELON ZANDAR

THE FEATURELESS, FULL-FACED mask – the hue of pastry – the wild hair seemingly made of nylon, the fingers fused together on each palm, giving him hands like crab claws: it was an agent of Tremelon Zandar.

The crackling sounds of fire, shadows of flames dancing over the side of the ice cream van plastered with vinyl stickers, advertising "Melded brain ice", "Fruity Tootscream" and "Lemon Foolsyouare".

From the serving hatch of the van being steered without a driver, the agent held a cardboard cone to a silver machine's nozzle. He pulled a lever and ice cream oozed in a spiral into it and on top of it. The agent took the ice cream-topped cone and placed it in front of his blank mask as if scrutinising it. Then he held it at arm's length out of the serving hatch. Stave looked with alarm from the window of the bus, and heard a staccato voice coming from the van.

'You. Don't. Want. This.'

Somehow, Stave knew that the agent meant the opposite.

There was something indefinably dreadful, a shuddering horror, about this simple act. Stave's throat dried as though the noxious, gassy smell of refuse had returned.

The agent of Tremelon placed the cone, slowly and precisely, into a holder on the small counter, flicking his head from Stave to the ice cream, then back again. His right claw hand disappeared below the counter. It appeared again gripping a blowtorch. The splintering sound of breaking branches, or bones, heard even from outside over the roar of the engines.

The agent turned a milled ring on the blowtorch and lit it with a lighter held in the other clawed hand – a blue flame spurted from its end. He brought the flame closer to the ice cream while nodding.

Intimidating. And yes, I am intimidated. This is personal somehow, I know for certain. My brain is fogging more and my tongue is twitching involuntarily.

Stave let out a cry and quickly walked the length of the bus once more to the driver.

'You've got to slow down, now! You can't beat the speed of the van.'

Already the engine was labouring and the bus vibrating.

'Not allowed to talk to customers while I'm driving, told you that before. Creamy mash, burn and slash.'

'Burn and what? Listen now, you don't understand. That agent out there is part of a dream going bad, and it looks like he's after me in particular.'

Stave began to pant, clutching his chest which had tightened.

'I can't change speed for an enemy or even a friend for that matter. That's against company rules,' the driver replied. 'Anyway, someone's after you, you say. Everyone has an enemy, don't you know. In kindergarten, I was poked and prodded to distraction. Often had my head pushed into the sand pit. At school, my lunch boxes were stolen for a week. I was forever being kicked and punched. Worked in a cement kiln once. One morning, coming to work, the kiln was fired up. A small inferno inside, like a huge glass-blowing furnace or like the red rivers of molten lava in the crater of a volcano. Remnants of my car in there, in that kiln.'

A quick snapping of reality. Unreality overtaking again, a peculiar swamping of consciousness, as if by a flood of water or a subtle and undefined roaring of a wind.

The dream wind. Losing concentration again. Am I lost in someone else's dream? Still unsure.

The bus driver continued, 'At least, I think it was my car. It had been stolen the day before. The ones who did these things are different people but still the same – the common enemy.'

'A bit far-fetched, isn't it, a car left in a cement kiln? Don't they have foremen, labourers and management? That's a lot of people to convince to put a car into a kiln.'

'I didn't possess a car to drive for a week, rain or shine. Doesn't that prove something?'

I would walk for hours in the rain. Or sing in the sunshine. Do I remember that? Memories snatched as if by a thief of the mind, the moment they are brought to the surface of thought.

The driver sighed, sounding like the rattling of an exhaust.

'You could be right, I might have been mistaken on that one. I think that was a nightmare. Like the agent out there, a part of the nightmare; army of darkness. Out of the dark, into the blue. Telephone, crunching bone.'

'But whose nightmare? Already you seem affected, coming

out with strange sayings. This could be becoming your nightmare.'

'Yours, mine, good, bad, does it matter? Don't look at his face, I'll tell you that much. I might dare though, when I'm ready. Was taught that one by my colleague back at the bus station.'

'But there's no face to be seen. He's wearing a full mask over it.'

Like a death mask if it had features.

'Auntie Maude, silver sword. Oh, you're alright then.'

Still the roar of the engine, the regular and fast pulsing of light and sound through the long tunnel under the river. But then, quite without expectation, the bus started to decelerate. The ice cream van overtook, seemed to slow as well, then hesitated before accelerating and continuing along the tunnel. The bus finally rolled to a stop.

'Thank you, that's appreciated,' Stave said with relief. The ice cream van became smaller and smaller as it raced into the darkening distance. The sounds of the jingle faded to silence.

The driver adjusted his cap, shaking his round head.

'We've run out of petrol. That never happens. The vehicle is checked every morning before leaving the depot. If there is a depot. That could be part of my dream too. Either way, this is an incredibly rare occurrence. Perhaps there's a leak in the petrol tank. I'd better put a warning sign at the back of the bus. We don't want any accidents, do we?' He opened the half door to his driver's seat and stepped out into the bus gangway between the rows of seats. He raised his voice as he spoke over the intercom.

'We seem to have run out of petrol. I will phone my

headquarters and they'll send some fuel or a replacement bus. On behalf of the South Yesteryear Bus Company, I apologise for any inconvenience caused. I'm sure this positive dream experience will continue as soon as possible.'

The two other passengers looked up at the driver with varying expressions but both remained silent until Mariella called in a loud voice from the back seat, 'This is not good enough. What about my collection? I'm already late as it is.' She held up one of her painted wooden fish, cleverly articulated.

'I'm in no particular rush,' Quikso Lebum said, handling his bottle of champagne.

'I'm onto it now,' the driver stated, holding his mobile phone in the air for all to see. He retired to the driver's cabin. There was silence inside and out, except for the indistinct mumblings of his conversation.

Stave sat near one of his travelling companions, Quikso Lebum, as he adjusted his eye mask again. The mask now had intricate swirls of colour upon it.

'Do you know your eye mask changes design at random?' Stave remarked. The young man remained silent. 'Typical, isn't it,' Stave added, to engage him in conversation. 'If I knew what time I was due wherever I'm going, I'd probably realise that I am going to be late. Any idea of the time? I haven't got my watch on.'

'Digital or analogue?' Quikso asked.

Plagued with peculiar doubts concerning time. But a time for what? Or should that be when? This dream reality is playing tricks with time, I'm convinced.

'Does it matter?' Stave said.

'Not really, especially as mine's not working. I keep it for sentimental value. At least, I think I do.'

'Worth keeping then,' Stave said with a hint of irony in his voice. There was a tinkling melody, faint but distinct. It was getting louder. 'You'll be late for your gathering.'

'It goes on for a while, I'm told; they don't care what time I turn up.'

Stave looked ahead through the front windscreen of the bus and saw something white, growing in size, far ahead along the tunnel.

5: THE BUS DRIVER SUCCUMBS

STAVE STOOD WITH urgency. The insistent melody was the jingle playing from the returning ice cream van.

'I've got to get out of here,' he cried out. 'We must help each other; you have to help yourselves.'

If not, I will control you in a positive manner. I must. This is my dream going wrong, I have to believe that. Anything I think will become, I have to believe that now, too.

'You'll be lucky, without training,' Quikso Lebum said.

'You can hear my thoughts?'

'I didn't realise you were thinking. I heard you speak,' the youth replied. 'But understand this much, if Tremelon Zandar takes final control, we will have no say in our destinies. We'll be no more than beetles in a jam jar or specks under a microscope.'

'How do you know this?'

'The bus driver told me.'

Dread feelings of being boxed in, not just physically but spiritually too.

Quikso Lebum added, 'Unless we join forces, or so he said. But who would want to join forces with such bad people? The driver tried to convince me that a nightmare from

Tremelon Zandar can be good if we all embrace it.'

There was distress in Stave's voice, as he replied, 'Well, that's for him to think. He's already become infected somehow. As for me, I must leave this bus. And I would advise you to do the same.'

'You've got to go?' queried the youth. 'Well, nice talking to you. Please, take my business card.'

'You understand the urgency, but aren't worried? Thanks anyway,' Stave said, taking the card and running to the front of the bus. He glanced at the bus driver who was still talking on his mobile phone.

'One moment,' the driver said into the phone, then to Stave, 'Yes, can I help you?'

The van was getting closer still, becoming louder. Strings of dark blue smoke came from its exhaust pipe. The large plastic cone on its roof spun at a fast rate.

Stave said, 'Hurry, I want to get off the bus. Open the doors, please.'

'I'm not sure regulations allows that, sir. You have to stay on the vehicle until rescue arrives. We can't have anyone running about in tunnels, especially ones that rotate whenever.' He adjusted his cap and tapped the bus company insignia on the lapel of his uniform. 'I can always tell you a story to keep you occupied, now we've stopped. Heard you talking about decent nightmares. Here's mine, saves nine, perfect crime. I'm looking down from a rocky crag to a yellow beach in a cove. It's littered with sunbathers. They are tiny. I'm that far above, you see, I view them as no more than insects in a puddle. The sea is blue flames, rolling in and out like waves. That flaming sea hides burned and battered bodies underwater, laying on hardened lava shelves. They're the ones who've been taught the lesson. The sunbathers are making cardboard boxes for—'

'Enough talking, we need action,' Stave told him. Now the van was no more than four hundred yards away, the plastic cone on the roof flashing like a beacon, the jingle still coming from a metal grilled speaker mounted next to it. 'I demand to leave this vehicle. You see there, the agent of Tremelon driving that van, coming back towards us? I have the idea he's after me in particular, as I told you before.'

How could I make an enemy? Not that I can recall if I have friends or not.

'After you? After me too. No preferences, perfectly fair, no discrimination. Subtle dish, butter fish, bread cutter. So don't be selfish with your enemies,' the bus driver said, and he chuckled at his own joke.

'You're talking nonsense.'

'There are many of them, those agents – tall ones, short ones, a few with more arms than usual. I've often seen them with their ruffled backs to me, emanating blue smoke. Some have snakes coming from their heads. Impressive really, in its own way. One of them is there in the van with smoking metal pipes, coming for me as well. I've decided, he truly loves me.'

Stave said, 'Don't you mean he hates you? Enemies usually hate people they're after or at least dislike them.'

'He loves me like a lip-smacking dog licking a fresh bone from a carcass.' The driver licked his own lips, then said quietly, 'I've always wanted to be loved.'

Stave gulped and pointed, jabbing a finger towards the

windscreen.

'He's in our lane, driving towards us. What does he want from us, from me?'

'Everything?' answered the bus driver while adjusting his cap. 'Pay packet, house, gardening equipment, computer? You name it, he wants it. Your memories, life, soul – yes, your very soul. Reveal it, prod it, unravel it as if it were a ball of wool, snipping lengths here and there, suck it up like spaghetti. And what type of soul? A water, fire or stone soul, one to be tortured by memories of an abandoned life? Dog muzzle for your sun, cat box for your moon. Snuff out the light of the stars as easily as candle flames. Count five, burn alive.'

Stave sighed with exasperation.

'That's far-fetched again. Souls can't be extracted, sliced or diced, taken, or blocked from entering some ecstatic state of being. I think I need to relax and reconsider the situation. Perhaps he's a friend of yours. Maybe you're both playing games, vicious tricks for fun.'

'Could you be right? Look, the van ahead is slowing. No doubt you think he can help if I talk nicely to him? The agent without a face is waving, see there?'

Stave gripped the bus driver's arms.

'We've all got to get out. This is feeling ominously familiar. Something is grabbing my throat in an invisible grip and churning my guts. Warn the other two down here, and those strange ones upstairs.'

'So who's the hero, all of a sudden? Anyway, there's nobody upstairs. There is no upstairs. This is a single deck bus.'

'How can you say that? It's obviously a double-decker.

Never mind, I think you're losing it big time.'

Stave turned his attention to Quikso Lebum and Mariella Fortana, and he bellowed, 'Follow me!' He turned back to the bus driver and ordered, 'Open those doors now or I will.'

The driver shook his head and inexplicably held his cap to his head with both hands, and cried out, 'He's back in the driver's seat of the van. I'd advise you to turn away, he's taking off the blank mask. I'll find out what's underneath, I don't mind. The ultimate understanding of sublime evil. It can be enfolded, encompassed…'

Before he could speak further, Stave leaned over the driver's door and started pushing and punching buttons at random on a control panel next to the steering wheel. They suddenly seemed as complex as the controls for an aeroplane with row upon row of dials, knobs, and switches.

Stave continued to turn the knobs and flick switches until the bus driver exclaimed, 'Hey, what are you doing? You can't do that to company property,' and finally, the doors hissed open.

'Thanks for nothing,' Stave muttered then jumped off the bus, the curved wall of the tunnel close to his left. He tilted his head and peered around the large wing mirror to look at the van. He viewed the driver's seat but saw no one holding the van's steering wheel.

Intuition told him to look back to the bus driver through the opened doors of the bus. That man still had hands to his cap but his fingers had begun to fuse. His mouth was open with a look of aghast shock and his eyes were closed with wrinkled eyelids.

Stave turned away and went a short way along the channel

made from the bus side and the tunnel wall. Then he lay flat on his back and wormed across under the bus as if a mechanic. He stayed there, panting. His turquoise suit was going to get dirty but no matter – there was only one clear alternative: hide.

Or die? And once dead, die over and again at the hands and mind of Tremelon Zandar, who would pull strips of the soul from me, bit by bit, little by little, as if my spirit was no more than a cooked chicken?

There was a pungent smell of oil, grease, and fumes under the bus. He could feel heat coming from the exhaust pipe.

A fridge magnet made of pottery was attached to the undercarriage. It had moon and sun symbols with an inscription upon it, "Night and Day". Stave pulled the magnet and it easily came away, and three tiny, metal feathers fell onto his chest. He placed them in his trousers pocket with the one that had come from the apple. As he did so, there was the muffled sounds of footsteps from people walking above, along the aisle of the bus. Then the noise as if ten or more passengers were jumping on the bus floor at the same time.

Stave shuffled further under the bus towards the back end. He tilted his head and saw the bus driver bending, still with eyes closed, carefully placing an enamel warning sign and a traffic cone on the road. After that, the driver felt his way along the left wall towards the rear of the bus. Now he was crouching and balancing on one of his crab-like hands.

'I know you're there. What are you doing under my bus? Get out, sir.' Stave kept quiet. 'No use denying it,' the bus driver added. 'The regulations clearly state that no passenger should be anywhere near where you are. Gone too far. Hit with a bar.'

'Keep quiet – what is up with you? That Tremelon agent will hear us,' Stave said softly. 'Where are the other two?'

'If I dared to open my eyes fully I could tell you, though I heard them get off the bus as well.'

'What's wrong with your eyes? And why are your hands turning to crab claws?'

Promises of false salvation. Twisting of true belief.

'I've succumbed to the nightmare. I'll be given my mask. I will have second sight. You'll not believe what I'm seeing now. The scalding neon outlines of something incredible. When I am ready – when I've been prepared – I'll see again and be bestowed wondrous gifts. I fully understand now. Tremelon Zandar doesn't want to steal my soul. He borrows it, buffs it up, gives it a spring clean, then will give it back to me. Embrace the nightmare as a path to enlightened self. Gentle screams of love, he told me.'

Yes, but a love of what? This bus driver has slipped on the slope. He has lost the plot. Whatever the plot is or was.

The driver continued, 'As for my hands, simply a natural reaction to seeing a horrid sight that was merely a reflection of my own evil, which I must subjugate. Explained. Do you see?'

'Don't you appreciate how you're being fooled?'

'Who's the fool here and who's the fooler? Come out and join me on the journey of evil personified. Feel the heat, lack of beat. Enjoy the burn.'

'No way. Has he gone, the agent?'

'For the while. I can summon him if you want.'

'No I don't want you to do that. You'd better be telling the truth. I can't stay under here anymore.'

Stave came out from underneath the bus and stood but with his back bent, and head kept low. He dared to raise his head to look through the back window into the bus interior. As far as he could tell, it was empty.

'I've something for you,' the bus driver continued. 'From Screamy Dan.'

'Who?'

'Screamy Dan, my new friend, the agent. Weaker light, stronger darkness. It's a bit mashed up. I'd eat it before it melts.'

The driver showed him an ice cream, held between his wrists, some melting and running down the cardboard cone onto his fused fingers.

Stave took it on impulse and ran from the bus to the traffic cone, placing the ice cream in a hole in the top of it.

A cone on a cone. Seems natural.

Another gust of a dream wind. This time, more like a change in the atmosphere with another layer of reality taken away.

An origami bird fluttered from out of nowhere and transformed into a starling, the size of a dog, before flying down the tunnel.

A whispered utterance.

'Where you going?'

He turned to see Quikso and Mariella outside at the back of the bus.

'Ah, you're both there. Your guess is as good as mine,' Stave replied quietly.

The bus driver heard him.

'I hear you all, you know. Back on the bus, immediately. Feebly. Heebly-jeebly.'

'Come with me, let's all find a way out of here,' Stave said to the pair.

They both shook their heads while Mariella clutched her bag of wooden fish wrapped in newspaper and Quikso gripped his bottle of champagne.

'I'll find my own way out,' Mariella said and she looked insistent about that.

'Me too,' Quikso added.

'Well, if you're certain. See you, then,' Stave replied, disappointed. 'Take care, both of you.'

Far behind the bus, another origami shape fell. It was a simple, paper boat. It immediately transformed into a massive galleon, blocking the tunnel from the way they had travelled.

This is all getting more peculiar.

Without looking back, Stave climbed up onto a short wall and over the railing onto a walkway. He ran until he came upon a metal door inset into the curved wall, the word "Maintenance" painted neatly upon it.

Exit from turmoil, or entry to worse?

The concrete ribs either side of the tunnel had turned to huge, calcified ribs of some massive sea creature.

The agent of Tremelon had appeared again from behind his ice cream van and walked with determination past the bus. As he came upon the ice cream he snatched it from the traffic cone with a clawed hand and while striding towards Stave, held the blowtorch to it.

'Not getting any better,' Stave muttered, as he took hold of the door handle and turned it.

6 : FACTORY OF HOPE DEPLETING

THE SCRATCHED DOOR opened. Stave Swirler moved swiftly through, turned, and slammed the door shut. After clanging, it hummed like the sound of electricity running through a circuit. He was plunged into rich black with mauve amoeba shapes floating before him, projected from his retina. Fumbling onto one side of the doorframe and then the other, he found a switch. An orange-yellow light illuminated the small stock room. He put his ear to the door and, with one eye closed, listened intently for any noise from the tunnel.

He turned on his heels to view the room. There were aluminium racks lining two mauve walls, and piled plastic crates filled with equipment at the far end. On the racks were cardboard boxes marked "pending" in scrawled grey ink, and glass bottles, stamped with sinister designs, filled with blue and grey liquids.

He was trapped. The agent of Tremelon could come through the door at any moment brandishing a blowtorch, or worse, take his mask off.

There was nowhere to hide. No other exit for escape, an air vent in the ceiling too small to climb into, and nothing on the concrete floor except the crates and a toolbox. Stave had the idea of picking up a tool from the box to defend himself but considered that wasn't such a good idea.

Escape rather than fight.

The only alternative was to move the crates over to the metal door, in the hope that the weight of them would be enough to prevent the agent from entering. Stave began pulling stacked crates from piles, placing them on the dusty floor and dragging them to the door.

There was another door with a key in the lock that had been hiding behind the crates. Stave removed the last of the crates from this exit and opened it quickly, locking it on the other side.

He was presented with a large room, a clattering conveyor belt running the length of it, carrying flattened cardboard boxes from out of a swirling blue globe. At the other end of the conveyor belt stood a man dressed in overalls. He busily made up the boxes before throwing them into a square hole in the wall. It was protected by a mock fire made of red and orange paper flames blown by air.

On all four sides of the room were organ pipes striping the walls, of varying lengths and thicknesses. They peeped and tooted at random.

Stave ran up to the worker.

'Hey, what's this about?' he asked loudly, above the clamour.

'Can't stop at all, I'll lose the sequence,' the man said, continuing to make up the cardboard boxes from the flattened ones taken from the conveyor belt.

'There is no sequence – all of the boxes are identical. Can't you switch off the belt for a while? It's very noisy.'

'Look, out of my way, I work for a promise. Let me get on with it otherwise I'll be behind schedule.'

'What promise?'

'Do I have to tell you?' the man replied in a distraught voice.

'No, not if you don't want to.'

The stranger paused before saying, 'A promise of dream heaven, a beautiful cottage for my wife and I. Living a life of simple luxury. But before that, I have to finish this important job, the first of many.'

Ludicrous, a pointless task. And I can bet I know who set the task for him. He is being tricked.

'Don't you realise you are being fooled, like everyone else, who has an encounter with Tremelon Zandar or his agents?' Stave told him, as the tooting and peeping from the organ pipes grew in amount and volume. 'You mentioned a cottage. What sort of cottage? I'm sure I live in a cottage too, I'm certain.'

The man remained silent.

But when Stave asked him the whereabouts of his wife, he answered, after drawing in breath, 'They'll release her, won't they, when I've finished this task,' and he glanced to the high ceiling. Stave looked there also, to see a mass of blue pipes. 'Now look what you've made me do. I picked up the wrong flat box,' the man said with annoyance.

'But they're all the same, I tell you,' Stave answered.

'To you, they may be. To me, there are subtle markings to identify which one to pick up before the other.'

'So subtle they can't be seen. I do believe you've been hypnotised in some fashion. You are making identical boxes and throwing them into a theatrical fire, the same way. What differences can there be?' The agitated man refused to answer while continuing his futile and bland task. 'All I can say is, if this is your dream world, it's a drab one.'

At that moment, the pipes on the walls played the same jingle that had come from the ice cream van.

'I've got to go,' Stave said, sensing the agent was close.

Now the jingle played with more urgency, and Stave watched with alarm as the room filled with blue smoke coming from the ends of the organ pipes. The door that he had come through bulged, and blue spots appeared on its grey surface.

'I must get out of here and I advise you to do the same,' Stave said.

He glanced around. He noticed that one of the cardboard boxes thrown into the hole through the paper flames, slid onto a brass chute and disappeared from view. The only means of escape, he guessed.

Taking hold of the man's arm, Stave pulled him but he struggled, and released himself from his grip.

'Leave me alone, you're spoiling everything,' he shouted.

'It's not me spoiling everything, I can assure you,' Stave replied loudly. 'Please, don't be a fool, follow me.'

The man in the overalls held onto the edge of the clanking conveyor belt as if expecting Stave to pull him away again.

The jingle from the organ pipes became shrill and deafening. Billows of blue smoke were thickening. Both men coughed as it attacked their throats.

'We have to go. I can't leave you,' Stave cried out and he ran over to the man.

He nodded, finally convinced, and when Stave leaped into the mock fire flames and tumbled and slid down the chute, the worker followed shortly after.

7 : KEEPERS OF THE CHASM

AFTER A SHORT ride in darkness, weaving down the winding chute, Stave landed on a pile of cardboard boxes that crumpled beneath him. Many others were stacked neatly from floor to ceiling. There were skylights above, letting a diluted light penetrate the gloom.

Hollow and echoed metallic noises emanated from the warehouse above, mingled with the reverberating jingle from the organ pipes.

He got up with urgency and moved away from the end of the chute. Then he threw boxes in front of it, just before the workman fell from its end and landed on them. He stood, still coughing.

'You unhurt?' Stave asked.

'What's to happen to my wife now?' he wailed, ignoring the question.

Stave moved closer to him and put a comforting hand on one of his shoulders.

'I can't answer that,' he finally said. 'But I do know that if you had been overcome in the warehouse then there would be no possibility of ever finding her.' The man bowed his head. Stave added, 'In the meantime, we must find a way

45

out, then perhaps you can find your wife.'

'Yes, thanks, I hope so,' he said, as tears formed in his mournful eyes. 'Tacie is so fretful without me. I'm Konie, by the way.'

'And I'm Stave. Don't give up hope.'

They shook hands and after a pause, both surveyed the claustrophobic place. There were no doors to be seen.

The noises from above ceased.

There was stillness in the dimly lit room full of boxes, and a deep silence except for the occasional chirruping as if made by a grasshopper.

A sense of being watched. But no, there's no one else but us here, I'm sure.

Stave stood, motionless for a while, taking in the peculiar ambience of the place. Then, half hidden behind more piles of cardboard boxes, he noticed a sturdy wooden door with a stone arch above it.

'There, this way,' he said to Konie. They went over to it and after clearing boxes away, Stave turned the cast iron handle and pushed on the door. It opened a small way.

It's stuck.

'Give me a hand, will you.'

They both put their shoulder to the entrance, pressing their weight upon it. With a grating sound, it opened wide enough for them to slip through, then it shut behind them of its own accord.

They found themselves in a circular room of considerable size. The continuous wall made of cream granite soared upwards to a point, high above, like a massive teepee might. Around the room's circumference stood at least ten more stone-framed doors. Each had a massive, animated mouth upon it, moving with twitching motions while whispering.

Fascinating. Like the rustling of leaves.

In the centre of the stone tiled area was a cavernous crater, thirty feet or more in diameter. And placed equidistantly around its ragged edge were three figures with ebony faces, each one more than eight feet tall. All had long, purple beards, plaited and sculpted into the shape of an artist's paintbrush. The strange characters pointed to the crater, to each other, or upwards. They were miming to an unheard beat, a mysterious, mystical semaphore known only to themselves.

The first figure, dressed in a cyan tunic, had a sphere upon his long-haired head. The second man looked identical except his tunic was magenta, and the shape on his head was a cube. The third one, with equally long hair and a paintbrush beard, dressed in a yellow tunic, adjusted the pyramid balancing on top of his head. They created an impressive dominance in the room and all three gently glowed.

'Who are these incredible people?' Konie asked in a low voice, as if in reverence to their extraordinary and distinctive auras.

'I don't know,' Stave answered, 'though they seem benign enough.'

There's something special about these three giants.

There was a becoming fragrance in the still air and a modulated droning from out of the crater. Stave stepped boldly forward towards the edge of it.

'Go no further. Step back,' the giant in magenta ordered,

his voice deep and penetrating.

After a pause, the man in yellow said, in an identical voice, 'Let him look; let him try to understand,' followed by a third voice, matching the quality of the other two exactly, as if all had been the one person speaking, 'Maybe he should look, maybe he shouldn't.'

Stave was undecided what to do, then considered he should step backwards, away from the crater in this dreamy place, away from those strange attendants.

He was in awe of the three giants, feeling the urge to bow to them but he resisted the temptation.

'Perhaps we should leave?' he asked, looking up to their wise and ancient faces.

There was no answer from them. Again they started their silent gesticulations, with the large mouths on the doors whispering more urgently, and the droning from the crater sounding like a mass of violin strings and bells.

Stave took the silence of the giants as an indication that they should leave. He called over to Konie in a low and respectful volume.

'Let's get out of here.'

But which of the many doors had they come through? Did it matter? Should they use any one?

While pondering, the giant man in yellow appeared to understand Stave's predicament and he spoke, his bass tone seeming to tremble the air.

'You are weary already, unsure of yourself, and still your dream journey has only just begun.'

'Then that's what this is, a dream journey we're on?' Stave said. 'You can confirm that? So you must be a part of the dream cast, like the blacksmith and harlequin.'

The giant in the magenta tunic replied.

'We are unlike either of those. We are the keepers of the chasm.'

With that said, he pointed to the gaping crater in the floor, and strands of light emerged from it, seen to vibrate as if strings of an instrument being plucked.

All three giants spoke at the same time.

'We are the sculptors of blackness, of nothing. From out of nothing, something is created. The void made becoming. I am part of three. We are part of one.'

The giant man in the magenta tunic fashioned a paper bird from a sheet of paper which had appeared in his hands. The gentle sound of rain filled the room, though there were no drops to be seen. He threw the origami shape and it flittered into the chasm.

'What is this gaping hole?' Stave asked.

'Your questions cannot be answered here,' the man in the yellow tunic replied. 'You must find yourself to answer yourself.'

'With respect, you are talking cryptically,' Stave said. 'Can anyone help us?'

More urgent whispering from the door mouths.

The man in the magenta tunic spoke.

'We are as trapped as you are but in a different form.' He fashioned a boat from a sheet of paper, and like the paper bird thrown, it too was let go to fall into the chasm. 'We are the time manipulators,' he said.

Stave dared to step forward again to peer down into the great space.

The sides of the crater were in constant motion. They ran with streams of purple lava, flowing around jutting rocks that were constantly creating faces. Those visages smiled or frowned, or looked quizzical. Halfway down, Stave could see wreaths of coloured smoke, forming and reforming, covering and uncovering what looked to be the cells of a gigantic bee honeycomb. Each hexagonal cell was alive with movement.

By paying attention to any particular one of the cells, it would enlarge enough to cover the others. When attention was lost, it would reduce in size to its original dimensions.

'A dream engine,' Stave quickly said.

Now, why did I say such a thing?

'You remember that much well,' the giant in yellow said.

Stave continued to look intently at individual cells below, enlarging each time he did, to show a beautiful woman playing a piano made of some glowing material within a field of wheat; a nest inside a tree trunk, holding rare, colourful birds; a bus in a tunnel.

'Enough,' said the man in magenta.

'But I've just seen the bus I was travelling on.'

Konie went to Stave's side. He too looked down.

'I see my wife; there, can you see her too?' he cried out.

The thunderous voices of all the giants: 'We can only do so much within our time and space, constricted by the agents of Tremelon Zandar.'

Their sphere, cube and pyramid headgear began to emanate rolling clouds, looking like sea waves crashing onto a shore.

The impressive figure in the cyan tunic continued, 'Our realm has been infiltrated too. Like bedbugs in a bed. Like mould on fresh bread. Like a rash on healthy skin. Now it's time for you to leave. You have caused an upset.'

'I'm not sure how but even if we have, I can assure you it was unintentional,' Stave replied. 'And where to leave by; which door? And go where?'

All three of the imposing giants remained silent.

Climbing up the side of the chasm was the agent of Tremelon, gripping the rock face with his claws, purple lava running over them. A distinct smell of rotting food in the air, and the sound of an ice cream van jingle again.

The three ebony giants had transmogrified into petrified wood.

Stave glared at the agent with worry.

'Quickly!' he yelled to Konie. 'Let's go.'

He ran to the doors lining the perimeter of the circular room but there were no handles – no means of opening them – just those massive mouths upon them. And their urgent whispering became even louder, creating a dream wind, as strong as an ordinary wind. It buffeted and blew Stave closer to the chasm.

He grabbed onto the tunic of one of the wooden giants standing at the perimeter, and stared into the chaotic chasm with fear rising. The agent of Tremelon was climbing higher, his blank full-face mask beginning to gain definition of features.

Dread took hold of Stave as the whispered dream wind blew in hard gusts.

Konie was blown into the crater. He had desperately tried to cling onto one of the stone giants, but had failed; he fell, moving down in slow motion, as if sinking in water. The agent, who clung onto the chasm wall, lunged at him but missed.

The agent reached the top of the crater and without warning, a clawed hand clamped tightly about one of Stave's ankles. He yelled in pain from the vice-like grip as he was dragged to the lip of the crater. He tried kicking the agent but the grip was too strong, restricting movement of his leg.

Finally, he lost balance and dropped into the chasm. The agent began to take off his mask, ready to expose the horror which lay beneath.

Stave turned away, his limbs flaying as though a drowning man.

Then he discovered he could swim through the air. Like Konie before him, he moved gently downwards as if through the water of a lake.

He continued down into the airy chasm, his arms now waving gently, the shafts of light shifting and splaying about him. He could see the cells far below had sealed with what looked to be blue wax. He felt the agent's presence not far behind.

To his left, he spotted the opening of a large metal pipe leading from the scarred, lava-covered side of the crater. He air-swam to it and entered, and found his footing.

More whisperings from the plain curves of the tunnel. He stood upright and walked along it, avoiding old equipment – contorted typewriters and molten sewing machines amongst others – along his way.

The agent moved quickly along the tunnel behind him.

Stave broke into a run, finally coming upon an open sash window at the end: he climbed through it as quickly as he could and dropped down onto the pine floorboards of a noisy tavern bar.

8: SAND DRINKS ON THE HOUSE

'HEY, WHO LEFT that window wide open?' someone bellowed above the sounds of brawling. A man wearing a gas mask came over to Stave. 'Do you want to get caught as well?' he said, his voice muffled by the mask.

'Of course not. In fact, I've just escaped,' Stave replied. 'But he's still after me, though.'

'And your friend?' the man asked, indicating to Konie.

Stave nodded.

'Emergency measures,' the man in the gas mask continued while pressing a button next to the sash window. A steel shutter descended and completely covered the whole of the wall with a clunk. There was an advert painted on it for The Yesteryear Bus Company, along with their logo, and a line of type that read, "Gets you nowhere fast."

'That about sums it up,' Stave muttered.

The dulled voice of the man in the gas mask: 'What did you say?'

'The bus company. Ever since I've left the bus, I seem to be getting nowhere fast. Like here. Who are you, may I ask, and what is this place?'

Stave waved an arm at the tables and chairs that were half

buried in drifts of yellow sand. Opposite those stood a curved bar area with bottles and optics behind it. A few men and women stood with glasses filled with sand in their hands. Several more customers were cheering and shouting at two gas masked figures rolling over piles of sand as they fought on the floor.

Above them, a ceiling covered in grass; at the end of the sandy bar, an old woman was busy using spider webs to weave, every now and then brushing particles of sand from the delicate cloth on her loom. Beside and behind her were masses of cobwebs, larger than an adult, some even reaching the floor from the ceiling.

'This is the sanctuary,' the man finally said with a puzzled tone as if it should be common knowledge. 'Dream cast, wanderers, bad dreamers, the lost ones, all are welcome. I am the landlord of this fine establishment.'

'Why all the sand? And why are most of you wearing gas masks and what are those two fighting about?'

'Do you want all the answers at once or one at a time?'

If the man hadn't been wearing a mask, Stave was certain there would be a wry smile on his face.

'I'm not fussed,' Stave said.

'As to sand, I don't see any. I'm not sure why you say that. Builders' sand, sea sand, gypsum, coral sand, what sort of sand are you seeing?'

Stave looked down and kicked at the yellow particles with his leather shoes.

'This sand, here. Oh never mind,' he said.

'Then I won't mind. But you should mind, you and your friend, not wearing a gas mask. You should care.'

'Why is that?'

'The agents' gas – their blue smoke. Highly toxic, don't you know.'

'I know as much,' Stave said. 'We've already experienced it at first hand.'

'Having said that, we haven't had an attack here in the pipes for quite some time,' the man said, waving a hand in the air. 'They tend to leave us alone to our own devices until…' he tapped the fingers of one hand on his chest.

'Until what?'

'Until the calling. See that portal over there?' The man pointed to a glowing blue disc – the size of a dustbin lid – hovering at eye level by one wall. 'Where it goes when it's chosen someone, nobody knows. Who it decides to choose – to swallow up – is beyond me. It chases certain people like a bad-mannered dog and doesn't let up until it devours them. Then they're gone.'

The brawling had ceased. The two men who had been fighting on the sand piles by the bar, stood. Then they brushed sand from each other in camaraderie, and finally shook hands.

'They seem to have made up,' Stave said.

'They were fighting over a pint. Plenty more here, I told them, but they wouldn't listen. Still, as you say, all finished with. Would you like a drink?'

Stave was thirsty, after all.

'Thank you, I don't mind if I do.'

'And your companion?'

Konie shook his head.

'No thanks, I'm looking for my wife. Her name is Tacie.'

The landlord ignored him.

'Brandy, sherry, wine, ale?'

'A glass of red for me will be fine,' Stave replied.

The man traipsed across the piles of sand, kicking some into the air or onto the few floorboards showing, and went behind the bar counter. There, he used a corkscrew on a brown bottle and finally popped the cork. He poured sand into a glass and parked it in front of Stave.

'Bottoms up, on the house,' the landlord said.

'Is this a joke?' Stave replied.

'I'm not sure why it should be.'

The man put his head to the side.

'This is sand. Who drinks sand?'

'Back to your sand again? Here, I'll see if there's any sand in it. Let me take a closer look.'

The man removed his gas mask. He had no features, just a blank head like an egg.

'Whoa,' Stave let out, and backed away.

'What's the matter now?'

'Your face, what's happened to your face?'

The landlord grunted.

'Another of your sand tricks is this? Nothing wrong with my face.'

'You must be dream cast, I'm guessing.'

'I have my own dreams, thank you very much. Like the one where I'm living in a beautiful cottage set in a wonderful landscape. And—'

'Not you as well…that's not a dream, it's a reality. The only reality I remember now. You've been given my memory, I'm certain, what little there is left of it.'

'More sand tricks,' the man without facial features said.

'No tricks, just lost,' Stave replied.

For some unknown reason, a shiver of coldness enveloped him.

Konie had been conversing with the men and women holding their glasses filled with sand, asking them if they knew where his wife could be found. None of them knew. Now he spoke to the old lady at the end of the bar, who weaved cobwebs in one of the corners.

'She's approximately five feet six, thick blond hair tied back, never wears lipstick,' he was saying.

The old lady did not speak but gently shook her grey-haired head and continued her weaving.

Konie heard his wife's voice.

'Is that you, dear?'

It came from behind a mass of cobwebs. Konie leapt over to them and frantically pulled them apart to discover his wife behind, sitting on a stool. She jumped to her feet.

'Oh Konie, I thought I had lost you for good. I've been frightened so I've been hiding,' Tacie said, and flung her arms about him and hugged him.

Stave saw this from further along the bar.

'Congratulations,' he cried out.

All the patrons raised their glasses and in unison said, 'Cheers,' some dream cast pulling their gas masks away to drink their sand.

At that moment, the glowing blue disc began pulsating and sending out filaments of blue smoke. The landlord donned his headgear once more, as did some of the patrons.

'I was convinced it wouldn't last; knew it was too good to

be true,' he said loudly.

The disc hovered close to the faces of those assembled, one after the other, as though inspecting them. They seemed unconcerned and continued their conversations. Perhaps they knew the blue disc was not for them…

As it came closer to Stave, he made his way between the customers to move away.

The pulsing from it increased in rate and Stave could smell refuse, a deep and disturbing aroma clinging in his nostrils.

He turned to run as it neared him but accidentally bumped into one of the sand drinkers who said, through his gas mask, 'Hey, calm down!'

He pushed Stave in the chest. Stave lost his balance and fell onto the bar. It crumpled as if made from polystyrene. He reached out to hold onto the back of a chair but that did the same – he easily snapped it.

'Don't fight it, dear,' the old woman called out as she pushed the shuttle across her weaving.

Stave ignored her and ran around the far corner of the bar. But there were no exits to be seen. However, there was a large food lift – a dumb waiter – set in one of the walls.

He pushed plates of sand from its shelf, then climbed in.

Just as the blue disc hovered by the lift, Stave pulled on one of the cables, but it snapped; so did the shelf he was sitting on, and he dropped into darkness.

9: WHERE TIME IS STOLEN

STAVE FELL HEAVILY into a large mound of silver sand. Half buried in the sand were broken hourglasses.

Always falling downwards.

He lay there for a minute, winded, before getting to his feet. Then he walked furtively along a plain corridor lined with brown cardboard boxes.

What is it with all these boxes everywhere I go?

At the end of the corridor stood an opulent and wide staircase, sweeping in a gentle curve. A long staircase too, with the end of it far down, disappearing into a haze. On each side were wooden carvings on finials, alternating with lit carriage lamps. The well-executed carvings were of boars, bisons, and beagles amongst others. On both sides of the banisters, the high walls were hidden by more stacks of cardboard boxes.

Shafts of clear, white light came from windows in the lofty ceiling and they picked out floating specks of dust that moved in strange patterns.

The plush carpeted stairs were littered with broken clocks. Grandfather and grandmother clocks lay with their backs broken. Mantlepiece clocks of all designs and types, pocket or wrist watches mangled, or their clockwork exposed, were scattered about them. He kicked cogs, levers, and springs out of the way as he walked carefully down the stairs, avoiding wall clocks, chronometers with their glasses punctured, and even the occasional thermometer with its glass tube smashed, leaking mercury.

He felt compelled to count the steps as he made his way down, walking with care about the debris. A pungent odour of decay hung in the air. The wall far ahead of him peeled grey paint in shadows, strung with thick cables.

He had been glancing behind to check he wasn't being followed. After a while, he decided all was as well as it could be.

I seem safe. I hope Quikso and Mariella are safe as well. I've no choice but to carry on.

Perhaps he could consider his situation as adventure, no matter it was a bad dream nor one not much set in reality. Indeed, that surely could be an advantage.

Halfway down the stairs, something caught his eye. Lying between the scattered clock wreckage was a miniature ladder. Stave bent his back to study it. The wooden object looked interesting and after picking it up, he put it into his pocket with the four metal feathers.

He continued treading down, finally discerning the end of the staircase ahead.

On the penultimate step of the staircase, grey paint on the carpet formed the words, "draw the line here". And a violinist stood upon the final step, wearing a smock and leggings. He rasped and scraped his bow over the stringless neck of a violin that he held under his chin. Then he paused to say, 'Seek the light, beware the darkness.'

'I'm trying my best,' Stave answered. 'Don't you see you've no strings on your violin?'

'I hear the music in my head. Can you hear it too? When I played in concert halls, I reduced audiences to tears with the sheer brilliance and beauty of my sublime sounds.'

'I can well believe it but I can't hear your music, sorry.'

'No matter. One day you will listen to the music of the spheres. When the adventure starts again.'

'What adventure?' Stave asked with interest.

The man did not answer but instead began once more to scrape the bow across the stringless neck of the violin. Tears formed in his sorrowful eyes from the lament that only he could hear.

Stave walked a step towards him and continued around him. Glancing back, the violinist was nowhere to be seen, only his stringless violin and bow remaining amongst the scattered clock pieces.

At the bottom of the staircase, Stave stepped onto a steel bridge that spanned large pipes, with ducts below them covered in silver-coated insulation. There were the sounds of rushing liquid, groaning and creaking, metal shaking and rattling. He peered over the bridge railings and down into the half-light. Below him, one particularly large pipe with other smaller pipes along its length looked like a massive, many-legged insect. He inspected it with suspicion: the ways things were happening lately, he almost expected it to scuttle off but it remained still. Next to it ran a wide walkway. Up at one end of the walkway stood a brass lamp, its wick burning brightly, sending yellow light out to highlight double doors to a lift. The lift doors hissed open, with the lift inside suddenly dropping from view. A few seconds later, it appeared again. It was obviously out of order, with the noise of fizzing electricity, and sparks emanating from the bulb inside. It would be dangerous to use, he considered.

He continued along the bridge. Halfway across it was an aluminium ladder with a railing each side, leading down to the walkway. As he reached the ladder, he heard a voice coming from below.

'Hey there, I hear you making a racket up there. Are you part of the maintenance crew? I doubt it, foul breath, deep growl. Come here, this instant. That is a command.'

10 : TWISTED SOUL AMONGST THE PIPES

AFTER CLIMBING DOWN the aluminium ladder to the walkway, Stave confronted the person who had spoken.

'That's better,' the man said, holding the lapels of his uniform, his head lowered so that his cap cast a shadow across his face. 'What do you think you're doing? Only staff are allowed here in the pipes basement. I'm guessing you haven't even got a name badge.'

'I found this place by accident. By the way, there's something wrong with your lift,' Stave said, noticing then that the maintenance man, standing with his hands behind his back, didn't have any teeth.

'So you've come to repair it?'

'No, I'm down here to escape,' Stave answered, adjusting his silk tie. 'Sorry but I'm being chased. At least, I think I am, still.'

'Who's chasing you?'

'A glowing disc and an agent of Tremelon Zandar. He's after me with a dangerous weapon – a blowtorch.'

The maintenance man shook his head and licked his gums.

'He's just trying to scare you. It's just for fun, that's all.

And if you're talking about the Tremelon Zandar I know...'

He threw glances to the left and right.

'You know him?'

'I thought everyone knows him. At least, eventually. I've only had glances, indications, a taster. Helpful, thoughtful and kind to those who will give unreservedly. His nightmare to embrace via his agents is a test for the wondrous screaming dreaming to unfold.'

'I recognise your voice now,' Stave said.

The man lifted his head. Stave saw him with closed, wrinkled eyelids and a generous nose. The bus driver.

A hissing, and shadows moving over the pipes beside the walkway.

'Ah, and I thought it was you, the young man from the bus,' the driver said. 'I can see your neon outline clearly now; I recognise your life force. Very strong. Let me help drain it. Consider it a spiritual evacuation. On the house.'

Stave stared with bewilderment at the side of the man's mouth: a small scar there wriggled like a beige centipede.

'Keep away. And steer clear of my soul. Aren't you aware of the fact you are going slowly mad?'

Beyond help, outside of Stave's capacity to assist…

'Then it's a delicious liquorice of a madness,' the bus driver answered. 'Flavoured with the grey and blue to find the true sanity, my friend.'

'Then I'm no friend of yours.'

'Don't you see? Can't you try to understand? I have embraced the subtle recruitment, drawn the line between good evil and bad evil. My hands will be replaced – in fact, eventually, all of my body parts will be replaced with wonderment, to be the container for my newly cleansed and repaired soul. Give your bad evil in your pumping heart to the one and only Tremelon Zandar. Come, let us dance.' The bus driver lurched forward, holding out crab hands that flapped feebly on the ends of his plump arms. 'The dance of death of what you thought you knew, to a new life of vision and understanding.'

His Adam's apple moved up and down as if in a spasm – he regurgitated an egg. It dropped from his saliva-wet lips to the ground and broke into two. Tiny snakes ran from the eggshell and dispersed.

The clanking and slithering shadows increased from below. Then, without warning, the ice cream van jingle echoed about the concrete-walled place.

Stave leaped away from the former bus driver who had become the maintenance staff member and ran behind him. The man turned surprisingly quickly for an older person and walked resolutely towards Stave, who walked backwards towards the damaged lift inset into one of the grey walls at the end of the walkway.

'Have a dance of whirling cloud, spilling your deep centres. Or accept and let the agent of Tremelon knock some clean sense into your silly, slow brain, with a blowtorch.'

'You really have lost it big time,' Stave shouted, feeling hot all at once. 'He's after every ounce of me; mind, body and spirit, I understand now. He's a virus, trying to wriggle his way through my being like he's doing to you. You've been blinded in more ways than one. As for the blowtorch, that'd damage me in a big way, for certain, then my temporarily anaesthetised soul would be stolen – molested or worse.'

Nausea feeling its way through my being…

'He infiltrates spirit in a positive cause. There's no need to fear him. If you don't consider a blowtorch part of an exquisite pain, then why not a hammer blow? Short and sharp, maybe to your ribs. He can play them like a xylophone. A rib at a time with a metaphysical hammer. Can you feel your ribs?'

For some reason unknown to himself, Stave complied by touching his chest. He felt numb there, no feeling in the tips of his fingers either.

'You're affecting me already, get away,' he shouted.

'By removing your physical mass, piece by piece, joint by joint, you will eventually find a weightless haven, a world filled with permanent wonder and deepest enlightenment. Now, you come with me this instant,' the maintenance man ordered and while holding his claw hands out again as they snapped together and apart like pairs of scissors, continued, 'We'll see if we can't sort this out. Let me take you down the dark lanes via the grey shadows towards the frenzy of blue light. Give up the fight, sublime fright. You really are far too awake for your own good, you know. You ought to be in the tubes, with the others.'

'I'm not going anywhere with you,' Stave growled and pushed his new adversary against railings which were beginning to sprout pipes.

Stave ran along the grubby walkway, the pipes continuing their hollow rings and tones. There was only one place to escape, he considered: the lift.

As it became level with the walkway, he dashed in, frantically pressing the buttons on the control panel. The light buzzed and fizzed above him but this time the lift remained stationary. The bus driver turned maintenance man walked casually towards him; he held the lantern which now threw out grey and blue light.

'Let us dance till blue death overtakes in wonderment of pain.'

A spirit corrupted by Tremelon Zandar, there's no doubt about it. Got to get away from him.

An oppressive load came upon Stave, a darkening, heavy shroud enveloping his mind. There was singing in his ears like tinnitus, the extraordinary noises from the pipes becoming louder.

The lift began to move down of its own accord, and he descended into the greyness of rattling pipes and ducts. Not wishing to see into the noisy gloom, he turned to the back of the lift and discovered another a pair of automatic doors. When at the bottom of the lift's descent, the doors opened and a flood of light lit the interior. And just before the lift made its ascent again, Stave stepped forward and out with determination.

11 : JOURNEY TO NOWHERE

HE APPEARED IN the midst of a throng of people on an underground train. They talked excitedly together until a station announcement reverberated through the air, "Please mind the doors" then they became silent. As the pneumatic doors shut with a hiss, the train jolted and slid into movement. The passengers erupted into conversation again.

Stave had found a space to squeeze into and leant against the closed doors of the train. To his left stood a bamboo cage containing three brightly coloured butterflies. They flittered in random patterns. Those people crowding about him swayed with the movement of the carriage, all one way, then the other. Some had eye masks on their sombre faces, some held onto straps that hung from the cream coloured ceiling. One person had an empty fish bowl in his hands while another ate an orange, the sweet and sharp citrus zest in the air.

So many here. Where are they going to? For that matter, where have they come from? I wonder if I used to commute.

How easily I have accepted a lack of memory, and lack of understanding concerning my strange predicament. Within the hold of a wakeful dream which swings wildly from bad dream to good then to bad again.

'Where does this train go to?' he asked a woman in the standing group.

'Why, the gathering, of course,' she replied gaily. 'I don't always wear this hat,' the woman added, and she stroked her feathered bonnet. 'It's in honour. Do you like it?'

'Very much. In honour of whom though?'

'You tell me. Are you going to the gathering as well, in your snappy turquoise suit and neat tie? And what a lovely pair of leather shoes.'

A constant rumbled rhythm of metal wheels on the track. Clickety-clack, clickety-clack, clickety-clack…

Stave looked down at himself. The suit was still perfectly tailored, with no marks or rips.

'Not that I know of,' he replied. 'But I know someone who is going. That's if he escaped, though. Quikso Lebum. Do you know him?'

'I know of no person called by that name. I use to know someone nicknamed Quicksand. Perhaps I'll meet Quillso at the gathering,' she said and gave a cheeky wink.

'Quikso,' Stave corrected.

'That's what I said, didn't I? If he manages to escape, as you told me. Escape from what though, the clutches of a woman?'

She laughed, sounding like the top end notes of a piano keyboard.

'Far from that – the clutches of an agent of Tremelon. Have you heard of him?'

She shrugged.

'Tremelon who? I don't know that name either.'

'Do you dream?'

'What do you mean, do I dream? I'm constantly dreaming and never wake up.' The woman seemed to lose interest all of a sudden and turned sideways in her space to ignore him.

Your ceasing of conversation is unnerving.

Stave turned as well, shuffling one hundred and eighty degrees, to look through the glass pane in one of the doors. As the underground train passed a platform, he saw wooden pallets stacked high with cardboard boxes, and bundles of flat cardboard being tied with rope by animated mannequins.

He was becoming claustrophobic with the immediacy of the other passengers. One spoke loudly to him – almost shouting in his ear – above the babble of conversations, with mild panic engrained onto his face. His cheek twitched involuntarily.

'You there.' The voice taught but refined. Stave turned his head to him and attempted to back away. The man stood too close; Stave could smell whisky on his breath.

Are you drunk?

'Drunk on the wine of life. How absurd it can be!' the man said.

'Can you hear my thoughts as well?' Stave replied, slightly annoyed.

'I don't know, can I? Can you hear me thinking? I hope not. I have some pretty unsavoury thoughts sometimes. They should be kept private, for all concerned. But no matter if you can. Just keep my thoughts to yourself, OK? Listen, I've lost my car, can you help? It was one of many parked under the Olympian Shopping Mall, but it's not where I left it. It's a silver and black Tissue Derigible. I'm terrifically fond of it.

It's terrible; there one minute, gone the next. Somebody moved it to a different bay for a laugh, maybe.'

Another gust of dream wind, although this time it seemed like a scented breeze.

'I wish I could help,' Stave replied, 'but I don't know where your car is. I don't even know where the shopping mall is. I did think I might be going there at one time, earlier today, but I'd rather be going home, somehow, somewhere. Perhaps someone stole your car? These things can happen.'

The passenger narrowed his eyes as if he were in need of spectacles.

'You could be right. I have to find it. So they stole it and drove it to somewhere else? This is not what I was expecting to hear. I hope they don't look in the glove compartment. There's something very personal and special there that no one else is allowed to see. Salted olive?'

The man held out a greaseproof paper bag filled with them.

'No, but thanks for offering.' *My mind is acting in a strange way, with this forgetfulness. Have I stolen a car? Would I have done such a thing? Am I in purgatory? That's a possibility. Surely I've done good deeds in my life. But what if my deeds no longer remembered have been terrible? Do I forgive myself, now I have forgotten them? Illogical train of thought. Of course I wouldn't have stolen anything…* 'I do hope you do find it. Where are you travelling to?'

The man furrowed his brow.

'Somewhere else.'

Clickety-clack, clickety-clack, clickety-clack…

Other than where you are. Can you believe you live a waking dream? Or do you insist you're in your bed asleep, your mind here, your body there? Or do you reckon you can't awaken to a more real state than this real state because you are already awake?

Stave's attention was diverted from the conversation and his thoughts by a squealing of the underground train's wheels. He looked out of one of the door's glass panes again, to the murky walls outside of the rocking carriage. Now the train moved at a gentle, slower pace. There were alcoves chiselled out of the granite-grey tunnel sides. Illuminated within each were household items such as a bedside lamp, a bottle of milk, and a pair of yellow gloves.

The other passengers appeared to be talking nonsense with animated features and forced smiles, all still swaying with the movement of the carriage, as the train increased speed again.

Clickety-clack, clickety-clack, clickety-clack…

Stave gently pushed his way through them to the aisle of the main carriage and was surprised to find that all of the seats in the compartment were empty of passengers, save for one. Most of the seats – on both sides – were covered with convoluted tree branches. The tree roots, like chunky fingers, disappeared into the metal floor. Snails, the size of fists, were held in their twigs and embedded in the vertical, green poles. At the end of the carriage, the twirling wood reached ceiling height, tendrils finding their way around the strip lighting and along the studded seams of curved metal panels. And hanging at random on the clusters of wooden stems were beautifully-fashioned, silver coat hangers. He inspected one: it had been carved into intricate patterns and engraved with tiny icons.

The young lady from the bus sat amidst the tangled and

entwined branches either side of her, contentedly inspecting one of her wooden fish as if reading a book.

'Hello,' Stave said with pleasure at recognising her, 'you're Mariella Fortana, aren't you? We met on the bus. Glad you escaped. Is Quikso Lebum with you?'

She looked up. Her face had become painted with a chalky white paste, with a single black spot above the deep red of her lipsticked mouth. Her mahogany-coloured hair was now blonde and without her pigtail. She gripped the wooden carp firmly.

'You can't have it,' she said matter-of-factly, clutching it to her chest.

'I can't have what – your fish? I don't want your fish, really. It's a perfect sculpture but it's yours. I wouldn't dream of taking it from you. It would look nice suspended from one of the hangers though, to display it. It'd be like an unusual gallery exhibit or a unique mobile.'

'My fish haven't got hooks so I can't hook them. I've studied them enough to know that,' she replied with an unexpected sadness in her voice.

'Surely they have.' *All of your fish have hooks.* 'The one you're holding, there's a hook on the back of it.'

'Well I never,' she exclaimed, 'That wasn't there before,' and she stood, and hung the fish onto a coat hanger dangling from one of the branches. 'Thank you, whoever you are.'

'Stave Swirler. Surely you remember me from the bus.'

'What bus?' she answered, genuinely puzzled. 'Oh, that bus. But thank you, Mr Swirler, that looks really lovely. It shall remain there until I reach my destination. Yes, I remember you now. On the bus in the tunnel. That seems months ago. Are you going to visit Alicia at the gathering as well? Are you a dream instructor in training?'

She gave a becoming smile and for some reason known only to her, held her hands level with her face.

The miraculous in the mundane. Where did that line come from?

Stave said, 'I did consider I was going shopping at the Olympian Shopping Mall, on the outskirts of a city. But don't think I am now. Perhaps I need to find my cottage.'

'You have a cottage?'

'As far as I remember.'

'How wonderful,' Mariella remarked with sincerity.

Clickety-clack, clickety-clack, clickety-clack...

'How did you get here from the bus? How did you escape the agent of Tremelon?' he asked.

She creased her forehead in concentration.

'Ah yes, the bad guy with the hidden face kept on trying to take his mask off but every time he did, Quikso kicked him in the shins. Quite easy really. He eventually vanished. Don't know where to. The bus driver was acting in a peculiar way. He kept wanting to dance, but we wouldn't let him near us. At one point he was chasing us around the bus, his strange lobster hands–'

'Or crab.'

'–crab or lobster hands out in front of him. Eventually, two men arrived in a truck. They opened the engine flap at the back of the bus, one holding a funnel and the other with a gallon can. Filled the tank with diesel, I think. They said they were from the bus company head office and demanded that we abandon the vehicle, as they had to drive it to the nearest garage for repairs. Strange to think it needed repairing after it had only ran out of petrol. They did keep on flicking their heads towards the bus driver as if passing some silent message to us. The driver was argumentative and strangely creepy. Wouldn't open his eyes. But eventually, he agreed to let us go. And when the bus was in the distance along the tunnel, Quikso and I set off to find the next dream exit.'

'Dream exit?'

'We are heading deeper into the dream, aren't we,' Mariella continued. 'But just before we started walking, the bus driver gave me a rosette; you know, the sort given for horses at gymkhanas or dogs at showgrounds. A rosette with deep grey, voluptuous petals, and two streaming ribbons. Identical to the one Quikso has. I quite like it.

'Then we walked along the tunnel for at least a quarter of an hour. I was surprised we could breath the air but there were no exhaust fumes to speak of. It seemed very draughty all of a sudden though…'

'What did you do with the rosette?' Stave said, becoming agitated.

Without answering, Mariella nodded and placed a hand into her holdall, retrieving the grey and blue rosette.

'It's here. Isn't it beautiful!' she exclaimed, smiling.

The low-level conversation from the passengers standing by the carriage doors became louder all of a sudden, as Stave widened his nostrils.

'Throw it away,' he ordered, 'I think it's from a trainee agent of Tremelon. Aren't your hands burning?'

Mariella looked bemused.

'Don't be silly, my hands aren't burning for any reason. It's a thing of beauty, don't you think? See how the grey loops, like petals, are almost velvet. Delicious, deep velvet.' She placed the rosette to her nose and inhaled the heady aroma emanating from it that only she could smell. Her eyes widened and she laughed again in delight. 'The odours conjure red flock wallpaper and thick treacly wine, and closed-in, dusky, snuggle places. I'll pin it on my dress now.'

'Don't do that, you'll never get it off,' Stave insisted. But it was too late: she had pinned it to her marble-patterned dress. 'Ah, now you've been marked.'

'That's downright wrong of you to say. No one can mark me in my dream.'

This can't be your dream; it's my dream. Or maybe not. I'm beginning to doubt that.

Stave put his hands onto the rosette.

Mariella cried out, 'What do you think you're doing? Do you mind?'

'It's for your own good. I'll bear the pain of burning fingers and take it from you.'

'No you won't,' she said and she wriggled while Stave attempted to undo the safety pin attaching the rosette to her dress. His fingers were burning as expected but he persevered. The rosette would not move still nor was he able to rip it from the pin. The loops of material immediately appeared to be made of felt, then silk, then wool. He began pulling material – those forming the petals – from the rosette but they never decreased, for with each loop torn away and cast to the floor of the carriage, another appeared in its place. It seemed impossible to remove or destroy. Now the centre of the rosette was made of glass, then stone, then ceramic, then metal – like blackened iron – the whole of it, including the two strips of ribbon, the pin, and the material of her dress where it was pinned, melding into one.

My fingers are burning too much; can't bear the pain any longer.

He quickly pulled his fingers away.

'Mariella, I'm sorry.'

'And so you should be, trying to take what's mine.'

'I mean, I'm sorry I couldn't take it from you, for your own good.'

'Well, that's as may be.' She sighed. 'OK, you did enhance my dream with the hook. I forgive you. And you deserve something in return.'

'No, really, not necessary,' Stave said. 'And the hook must have been there in the first place.'

'Believe me, it wasn't. I've studied these beautiful carvings for days – as I said before, I would have noticed if they had hooks.' She took out another of the fish carvings and unwrapped it from its newspaper, turning it over to view the back of it. 'There,' she said, 'another one with a hook that wasn't there before. I bet all the others have hooks now. You are a dream sculptor, aren't you?'

'Not that I'm aware of. That's assuming this is a dream. People can't burn flesh and feel pain in dreams,' he said and inspected the blisters on the tips of his fingers.

Mariella shrugged.

'As I was saying, have these if you like them,' and she retrieved five tiny metal feathers from the bottom of her bag. 'I found them on the back seat of the bus.'

'Well, I do have some of those already; an odd collection

but I find them fascinating.'

'Then they're yours,' she said and handed them over.

'Thank you.'

Logic. Reality has logic – fixed rules and immutable laws, then why not a dream in reality? That must surely have a dream logic…

'What are you thinking?' Mariella asked.

'Not much. Except…look, I'm going to try an experiment, if that's acceptable to you.'

'No skin off my fish.'

He closed his eyes and willed with a command.

'Then I wish this carriage to slow down and finally stop.'

The underground train rumbled on.

Clickety-clack, clickety-clack, clickety-clack…

Well, that didn't work.

'Nothing happened,' Mariella said.

'Hmm,' Stave answered. 'How about the hooks?'

'What about the hooks?'

'If I somehow made them appear, then perhaps I can make them disappear.'

'Give it a go although it'll be a shame. I like the hooks.'

OK, the fish hanging from the silver coat hanger hasn't a hook anymore.'

Nothing.

I was wrong in my assumptions. No fish hook, that's all I asked.

The fish hanging from the coat hanger fell to the floor.

I see, the command has to be thought. Stop the underground train, now.

Nothing again.

Not strong enough yet. Could be that. Yet how can reality, albeit like a dream, be influenced just by thought anyway?

The fused metal rosette on Mariella's dress started to pulse with a grey light.

'What does this mean?' she said.

'My guess is, it means an agent of Tremelon is near. Or the rosette will affect your or my dream in a bad way. Actually, I really don't know. What I do know is, you need to unpin it, now, and fast.'

'You're so insistent. I will then, just to please you.' But as Mariella attempted to open the safety pin, her hands turned ice white and trembled uncontrollably. 'My hands – so cold,' she said, taking them away.

'I really don't know what to do,' Stave said.

Let the rosette drop to the floor.

The rosette remained pinned to Mariella's dress.

As she massaged her fingers to bring warmth back to them, Mariella Fortana spoke in a dreamy voice.

'So anyway, further along, we found another tunnel leading us to an underground train tunnel. That's a lot of tunnels. I could be wrong but there might have been even more tunnels, a whole labyrinth of them, worming their way under the river. Who knows what incredible engineering feats clever people have performed, hidden from everyday view? Tunnels for cars, tunnels for trains, tunnels for water, tunnels for chemicals; tunnels for this, tunnels for that, tunnels for mythical beasts for all we know. Green tunnels, covered in lush grass. That's what I needed to find…'

Stave paid no heed to the young woman. To him, it sounded like she bleated like a sheep.

He looked between the mass of branches at a window of the carriage. The alcoves in the tunnel walls were getting smaller and despite the articles displayed in them becoming smaller too, they seemed to take on a focused detail of their own. All about him was becoming dim as if the carriage lights were failing. The voices of the standing passengers had evolved to ominous creaking and metallic cracking, as if the twisted branches about him were cracking within the creaking of a large pipe. A strange scent wafted through the carriage, not unlike musky wallpaper, or treacly wine, or dusky places. As bilious as it made him feel, it had an addictive quality about it, a seductive ambience, as if one had to continually check the smell to confirm the impression of it over and again, never quite placing it. The small, lit items in the passing alcoves evoked a feeling of horror and dismay; they seemed organic as each one writhed and throbbed in a particularly detestable way in their tiny places. Stave felt nauseated and repelled by them.

As the train wheels became louder, Stave turned back to Mariella to avoid watching the passing alcoves with their miniature, hideous contents.

'The carvings are quite exquisite, aren't they?' the young woman exclaimed.

'Mariella, come with me. Do follow this time – I'll find a way to remove the rosette. This dream or reality is going bad again.'

Mariella looked bemused and so ignored Stave, even turning her head away from him and lowering her heavily-lidded eyelids, showing thick mascara on her eyelashes. On each closed lid was painted a fish eye.

She continued, 'Each scale is created in the minutest of detail and if one were to look at it with a magnifying glass, one would see more superb detail, as fine as hair. Look even further, teeth and nails, further still, blue smoke…'

A green silk curtain divided the carriage he stood in with the next. Perhaps there was safety in the other carriage. Stave attempted to pull Mariella by her arms to a standing position but she felt as heavy as stone.

As she gabbled on and the train wheels became louder still, Stave shouted above it all, 'If you can't come with me, I've got to leave you again, Mariella. I've no choice,' and he poked his head through the silk curtain.

He saw an empty carriage, devoid of people and any form of growth – no branches or plants of any kind – and in complete silence.

12 : FURTHER INTO DREAM TERRITORY

STAVE WALKED QUICKLY through into the next carriage and chose a seat at random.

He felt sure he was safe again. The atmosphere seemed immediately better. If only Mariella had come with him. He felt guilty at not bringing her but as she had refused, there was no more he could do to help.

He was relieved that the alcoves in the tunnel walls had gone. Now only sooty cables and the occasional light on the wall of the tunnel rushed by.

Clickety-clack, clickety-clack, clickety-clack…

The pattern of repetitive beats on the tracks was somehow soothing. His eyelids drooped and he was feeling weary and drowsy all at once. He decided to take a short nap before the train reached its destination, wherever that might be. Perhaps it would be the Olympian Shopping Mall, filled with shops of all types, bustling pedestrians hurrying past on the walkways and promenades.

At the same time that he closed his eyelids, a roar of laughter came from another carriage and his eyes sprang open again. Stave blew through his nose; perhaps his catnap could wait. Or perhaps not – as sleep tugged him again and he closed his eyelids once more and saw nothing but black with a dark blue shape creeping and slithering in the corner of his mind, another hail of laughter came from the passengers standing in the previous carriage. He shook his head with annoyance.

He looked to his reflection in the window opposite – a dark, slightly distorted image – and saw other reflections there, as if all of the seats each side of him were full.

Astonishing. Deeper into the dream.

There was the reflection of a man reading a newspaper and another talking to his partner, his mouth opening and closing like a goldfish. The reflection of a woman, next to his own – wearing bright earrings and a silver rose pinned to her blouse – looked to him and gave a brief smile as if in recognition.

Stave involuntarily checked the seat beside him but an empty place was all that he saw.

The reflection of the woman spoke.

'You are ebbing and flowing like the waves of a sea. Come, join us with our joyous company. We travel through dreams of all kinds.'

Stave heard the sound of tap-dancing or the flaps of a dog's ears when the animal shakes its head, or noise of tapping of fingers onto plastic. Whichever it was, he looked to the silk curtain dividing the carriages for some sort of explanation. studying it intently, as if expecting the maker of the source of the sound to walk, dance, or trot out.

Through a gap in the curtain, he glimpsed some of the standing passengers, now excitedly comparing rosettes.

A shadow on the floorpan. Stave looked up and to his left, and saw an inspector standing over him. A ticket dispenser on his chest was held by a leather strap about his neck. His cap seemed too large for him but this comical aspect was balanced by his serious jowls, suspicious eyes, and severe eyebrows.

'Ticket?' the inspector said in a clipped tone.

'Are you real or part of someone else's dream?' Stave asked.

But then what is reality? I can see this stout man as clearly as anything, fidgeting in front of me. If I poke him he would react. The same if I stubbed his toe.

'You are creating a conundrum with that comment,' the ticket inspector replied, then asked again, 'ticket?'

Stave bit his lip and fumbled in the pockets of his jacket. He extracted the small bottle of cough mixture from one and a business card from the other. He held the cardboard rectangle up to the inspector, then retracted it as quickly as he had offered it.

'I haven't got a ticket,' he admitted.

Guilty as charged. No ticket. But then I didn't ask to ride this train. And I didn't see any ticket machines.

'Of course you have, it's in your hand,' the inspector said and he took the business card, and held it close to his face. 'Quikso Lebum, Interior Designer and Official Gathering Guest,' he read. 'That will do nicely.' He appeared amused and upon clipping it with a metal clipping tool, he handed the business card back to Stave. 'That'll be fine,' he added.

Will it? Is it fine? Are you certain? It's not a train ticket and it doesn't even belong to me.

'Put the cough mixture away. Don't need it here.'

'You are certain?' Stave said. The inspector merely nodded and began walking away as Stave pocketed the cough mixture. 'Hey, before you go, can you tell me where this train is going?'

'Wherever you want. Where do you want it to go?'

'I've decided it must be the Olympian Shopping Mall. Or the gathering.'

'Then make up your mind which one and that's where you're going,' replied the inspector and then he paused before saying in a friendly way, 'I've seen you a lot in my dreams,' and held his hand out.

Stave shook it and said, 'Pleased to meet you. Have you been a ticket inspector for long? Are you part of the dream cast?'

'Since this morning to both questions. And it's still morning, isn't it? Who is to know, buried under the earth in this tunnel, the way we are. A night sky above or a day filled with sunshine. Or a planet's surface devoid of humanity, everyone hiding underground in the tunnels. That would be good for business. I've always wanted to be a ticket inspector. Here, let me give you another ticket. I like you. You're a good sort.'

'If you think I need another ticket...'

'Of course you do,' the man replied and he turned a handle on the machine around his neck. With a whirr and a ding from a bell, a small, metal object appeared into a tray. The inspector took it and handed it to Stave. It was a miniature metronome, no more than three centimetres high.

'Thank you, but how do you know I'm collecting these dream finds?'

'I don't, but the dream does,' he replied and tapped the side of his bulbous nose. Then he stood up and waddled away, disappearing from sight into the next carriage.

As Stave pocketed Quikso Lebum's business card and the miniature metronome, the underground train was slowing, as was the tempo made with the wheels clacking on the rails.

13 : VISIONS OF THE DREAM BEYOND

A PLAIN, WARM-GREY underground platform slipped into view beyond the carriage window, with mauve porcelain tiles on the wall. And as the train slowed to a standstill with a screech from the brakes, Stave stood, ready to leave the train.

He froze in confusion. A sudden round of applause, sounding like waves breaking onto a beach, came from an unidentified source. This was followed by a whirring and grinding: the complete side of the carriage – hinged at the bottom, similar to a wide ramp from a ship or aeroplane – began to open. The side lowered quickly and landed on the platform with a clank. The strip lights set in the carriage roof decreased in luminance to nothing, leaving only a gentle glow remaining, painting Stave's surroundings as if tinted by moonlight. The glow came from lightbulbs along the top of the mauve tiled wall, casting their gentle light over the descended carriage side and into the interior.

Stave sat again, settled back into his seat, and moved his lower limbs to become more comfortable. He was feeling dreamlike again, gently smiling and nodding in anticipation.

Go with the flow.

It was as if he were at a theatre, with the expectation of an occurrence. This was confirmed by the tiles on the platform wall falling all at once onto the metal and glass of the folded-down carriage side, with an impressive crashing noise. A pair of crimson curtains were revealed. They billowed and trembled as if from an invisible wind.

Between the flat carriage side and the wall, a strip of the concrete platform showed. Rising from it were eggs, the size of heads, their shells the hue of liver. Stave felt oddly disappointed when those eggs submerged as the curtains opened of their own accord. Revealed was a wall of tightly packed, framed photographs. Those photographic images were shown in warm greys within wide, black frames. As Stave concentrated on any one picture, be it an image of a doll, a cat, or a horseshoe, it became blurred, out of focus with the others at the periphery of his vision. He blinked and rubbed his eyes. And as he did so, those pictures also fell to the floor, like the tiles before them, to reveal a large underwater scene showing beyond a thick sheet of glass.

Under the clear water intersected by sun rays, there were ridges and hills of crystal coral. These let out rainbow fans of light. Deep blue sprouts of weed swayed within strings of effervescence. Their pods were silently exploding, each time giving a miniature fireworks display.

Two brown horses trotted into view between the coral hills. Their manes, tails, and forelocks flowed and waved with the currents. Beads of air, as bubbles, came from their wide nostrils. The heavy beasts with solid haunches and long necks were admirable to see under he water. They cropped the weed, sometimes the pods disintegrating in sprays from their mouths.

Crystalline fish swam about and under the horses' bellies. Those fish were many-gilled, with translucent streamers and stems growing from their heads and scaled bodies. When any one of the fish turned from its profile, Stave saw that instead of round buttons for eyes they possessed human eyes, complete with lashes and eyebrows. Intelligence shone from them as they danced around and about the underwater horses.

Stave was captivated by all this. He wanted to clap his hands but instead stood with a bout of energy banishing his weariness. He climbed over a carriage seat and walked out onto the horizontal train carriage side, so taken by those beautiful features of the fish. He stepped over the litter of tiles, broken frames and glass, to the concrete platform strip not covered by the carriage side. He looked up to the line of glowing lightbulbs but then was quickly startled: at the same time as the curtains hurriedly closed, the side of the train compartment rapidly sprang back up into position, sending the debris on it catapulting into the carriage interior.

The underground train was going to leave without him. But he was comforted by the fact that as it began to be swallowed by the tunnel, it was leaving without most of the other passengers either. They huddled together at the far end of the platform, arguing and pushing each other.

All except for one other person that he saw still on-board. As the train slid past, picking up speed, he saw Mariella Fortana sitting alone, hanging one of her wooden fish onto a silver coat hanger.

I hope she's going to be OK.

Stave strode towards the large group of passengers, over

the remaining shards of glass and the occasional mangled picture frame, or broken tile, scattered on the platform.

14 : ARGUMENTS AND CONFUSION

HE GLANCED UP and down the platform, then shouted over their noise.

'Does anyone know how to get out? There doesn't seem to be any exits,' he said. 'Or do you know when the next train is due?'

One of the arguing group spoke up.

'No, do you?'

Before Stave could speak, another passenger gave the answer.

'Two days.'

Yet another replied, 'Two days? You've got to be kidding. I can't wait here for that long. The Olympian Shopping Mall closes on a Sunday. Anyhow, we'd all get hungry and cold.'

Another dream gust...

'There's a snack machine over there, bursting with goodness. It dispenses Wheaty Crunch, or is it Tweety Crunch?' someone said, and someone else gave a hysterical laugh.

A tall man wearing pince-nez spectacles pushed his way to the front of the group to confront Stave. He had the sleeves of his striped shirt rolled up to his elbows and wore two belts about his oversized trousers.

He cleared his throat and said with disdain, 'I don't see anything to laugh about. In fact, quite the opposite. Someone has removed my fine bicycle and wheeled it to somewhere else. I can't find it anywhere.'

Here we go again…

He continued, 'It's not only frustrating but also worrying. And all you do is talk about Tweety Mints and waiting for a train arriving in two days. It really is not good enough. Do something.'

He pushed Stave in the chest.

'Now look here,' Stave remarked with indignation, 'I'm not the voice of the news. And I didn't mention any of that. Whoever said it, probably saw that hoarding,' and he pointed to it on the wall, on the other side of the sunken rails. 'Subliminal reaction. You see, there, that advertisement for Tweety Wheety? Now leave me alone, whoever you are.'

'I'm none other than Dario La, you should know. The amazing fact that I invented the bicycle pump surely must not have missed your attention. The Penny Weather…'

'Do you mean the Penny Farthing? That was invented at half past three on a cold Wednesday morning.' Stave was feeling as absurd as the situation was becoming and smiled at his own humour.

'Are you trying to be funny?' Dario La replied quickly, raising an eyebrow and puckering his lips.

'I guess I am,' Stave said.

'Well, I don't find you funny. In fact, I find you the complete opposite. I have to get out of here and locate my bicycle, it's imperative. I'm fond of it. I've owned it for years.'

All attention was upon Stave to speak again. But his sight was drawn to the sunken rails in the pit. A stream flowed there, over the red tracks. Minnows darted about polished pebbles and rocks, and the white insulation blocks. The fish occasionally formed groups, making random letters of the alphabet – as ephemeral as a sand painting – before dispersing to arbitrary movements again. Leaves, silver twigs and broken pieces of picture frames floated and moved on the shimmering surface. Stave's reflection in the stream was joined by reflections from some of the others passengers.

'What's to see?' one of the group said.

'Water and pond life trickling down towards the right-hand tunnel. This is the reason that there won't be another train for at least two days, I guess. We'll definitely have to find a way out of my real dream.'

How easy I am succumbing to believe that.

'Your dream? What are you talking about? Are you mad?' Dario La said loudly, for all to hear. 'This is my dream. Here, meet Verla, Maurick and Natameil. I concocted them from my mind.' Three people within the group bowed. 'They are part of my dream cast. As for getting out, this is a sealed platform, as well you know,' he said brusquely. 'I demand you find a solution. I have to get my bicycle back. It's imperative.'

The other passengers murmured in agreement.

'And I've got to find my pooch.'

'I need to find a pearl. Like that one.'

The person who spoke pointed to a corrugated oyster shell under the stream water. It sprang open, showing inside a flat, red tongue with a patinated spherule upon it. The shell snapped shut then, making the sound of a briefcase being closed.

A female voice: 'And I have to get to the gathering.'

Stave inspected the line of twenty or more people with their bowed heads as they looked down to the flooded tracks.

'Do you know Quikso Lebum?' another man asked him.

Stave hunted for the business card and upon retrieving it, showed it to the man.

'This Quikso Lebum?' he said.

'No, that must be a different version,' he replied. 'But why do you ask?'

'Why do I ask what?' said Stave as another dream breeze played invisible games with his mind. 'It could be we're all in his dream – it's decidedly absurd at times. I'm sure mine would be more sensible.'

'Are you calling my dream absurd?' Dario La barked. 'I find that offensive. You didn't take my bicycle, did you?'

'Why should I have taken it? I possibly own one already.'

In my cottage? Village – and a town. Another sudden memory. Both somewhere that I'm very familiar with…

'It's not important,' came an interrupting voice, slow and measured. The figure, at the far end of the platform, stood with a rolled newspaper held high and a claw hand held to his chest. 'What is important … is that the lot of you get to where you need to go. You'll be warm and snuggly; beetle-jerking hot, trembling till you rot. But no worries, that's just the end of the beginning.'

A woman close to him shuddered upon inspecting the man's mouth. There were two rows of grey upper teeth there.

'Are you eating peppermints?' she asked, then gasped at

sudden recognition. 'You're another agent, aren't you. And you're crunching teeth. Have you been following me?'

'Keep away from him,' Stave called out. 'He's been infected; he's an agent of Tremelon.'

'I know, don't have to tell me,' the shocked woman replied. 'You won't catch me, you're limping,' she added to the man.

'Probably has a cardboard foot,' yelled Dario La.

'No, that's only for his enemies. Anyway, let me deal with it,' Stave said, and he marched up to the trainee agent of Tremelon who limped towards him. 'Where do you think you're going?'

'To enrich the lives of poorly souls,' the trainee agent replied. 'Show them the incredible wonders of the good evil understood. Tainted life, sharpened knife.'

'You're the bus driver again, aren't you. And talking rot still. Evil is evil. There's no such thing as good evil.'

'Tremelon Zandar understands the evil in my heart and can transform it into grey and blue. Here, take this as a symbol of his love for the evil in your heart,' the former bus driver said and, before Stave realised what was happening, the man had hung a cowbell on a ring around his neck.

'Hey, I don't want this!' Stave cried out and attempted to remove it, but burned his fingers. 'What have you done? Take it off, I demand it; I've no evil in my heart.'

But the trainee agent ignored him and limped away.

Marked. Like Quikso and Mariella with the rosettes.

Someone else spoke up.

'Don't worry yourself, it's just a present from a stranger. Agents of Tremelon don't look like that. They are short, with an extra finger on their left hand. That could be the reason why they are so awful. I heard one of them cut off the tail of a cat one time.'

'His name is Tremelon Zandar. He will make everyone's life a misery.'

'My unwanted adversary is called Tremelon. I'd recognise him anywhere. He's short and wide like a blue crab.'

'My version is slightly different. Trombone Zandibar, he is called. He's pure evil personified, and I shudder just to say his name.'

Arguments happened all at once, barking and braying, pushing of shoulders and thrusting forward of heads, each talking as loud as possible so as to be heard above his or her neighbour. The consternation and anger grew, the din they made echoing and amplified by the bare walls of the station.

'Wait, calm down everyone,' Stave shouted amidst the clamour.

With this spoken, one of the aroused fellows turned on one foot as if practicing a ballet step.

He yelled, 'Calm down yourself,' and then, without provocation, pushed Stave in the chest with a mixture of fright and confusion upon his face.

Stave toppled backwards, his arms flapping in an attempt to retain balance. He fell into the water-filled pit that was the railway tracks. And with a splash, the loudness of the bustling and fighting passengers became a quiet rushing.

He felt strangely comforted by the water about him.

15 : UNDERWATER DISCOVERY

HE QUICKLY HELD his breath. His eyes sprang open while sitting on the submerged tracks. He was about to surface when his attention was drawn to the aggregate that filled the gaps between the rails. On top of it were trinkets, the sort to be found inside boxes of cereal or Christmas crackers.

Dream summoning is needed so I can inspect them further. I summon some sort of breathing device.

A snorkel appeared on the aggregate.

That worked really well.

He took hold of it and placed it over his face.

Strange that I feel water on my skin yet not through my clothes.

He dug out some of the trinkets with his fingers. There were models of a goat, a soldier and a lute, all made from plastic, and even a magnifying glass. On one side of the rim of the glass was the word "obverse". He picked up the concave disc by its handle and held it to the objects, one after the other in the clear water. Looking through it, the magnified moulding of the goat was precise and accurate. He could see every individual hair of its coat. Even the tiny horns had a roughness over them like bark. The lute was strung with the finest of strings, and the tuning pegs were seen to be turned to perfection with delicate, minute curls carved into them. The marquetry on the body of the instrument was made with precision. The soldier's epaulets, cap badge and medals were clearly defined, as well as the regalia on the drum.

Beautiful models created with exquisite detail.

As he inspected the tassels on the rope hanging from about the soldier's drum, and a ladybird on the end of one raised drumstick, he heard a dull thumping as if the drum was being played. He instinctively held a hand to his chest and felt his heartbeat, and the repetitive thumping matched it. He turned to face the direction from which the muffled bangs came from but could only perceive clouds of algae and pondweed.

He turned back to see all three items he had viewed through the magnifying glass were now full-size – the goat, the lute, and the soldier with his head and shoulders sticking out above the water line.

Stave marvelled at this for a moment. How could that be possible? But then his reality had become a dream, after all.

He wondered if the opposite effect would happen, by turning the magnifying glass over.

He discovered that by turning it to its obverse side, it became a reducing glass: simply by looking through it again, it made the items small once more.

A useful find. A dream item in a dream world.

Glowing to his right was a row of fires, as tall as the height of water, their orange flames licking the floating microscopic debris. A fierce barrier, but he was compelled to swim through, all the same. The closer he swam to the fire barrier, the colder he got, and where the flames touched him he felt colder still.

Beyond the flames stood a door seemingly made of liquid, as if the water had become jelly and had congealed into its shape. Stave pushed on it and swam through. Onwards he went over the tracks, sometimes surfacing to see his progress along the tunnel.

Further on still, he came across a metal hatch under the water. He unclipped it and the drumbeat got louder. He opened the hatch and looked through it, down into the interior of a large boat. The boat's sides were as tall as an old wooden ship, great chunks of timber curving upwards.

At the transom end, an agent of Tremelon stood with his plain mask, turning over a sand clock gripped in a crab claw hand in time to his beating of a drum, the beater held in his other clawed hand.

Two rows of people sat along the length of the boat. Their feet looked to be made of cardboard. They pushed and pulled on oars. They laughed and talked contentedly as they did this, unaware of their final journey. Lost in their dream that, unbeknown to them, was becoming a nightmare.

There was no way to help them. Stave closed the hatch.

He had been clutching the magnifying glass all the while he had been swimming underwater. Upon placing it in a waistcoat pocket, he stood upright into the air of the dimly lit station, the flowing amber water of the track stream now just below his shoulders.

When he had taken off the snorkel, he could see the same station platform with the same passengers, although they had stopped their squabbles and were in an orderly line again. All of them stood still, with their heads inclined to the source of regular noises and disturbed water. Splashing sounds emanated from the tunnel at one end. It sounded like oars put heavily into the water or the surface being beaten with paddles at a constant rate. Hissing and growling too.

'Get out of there, you fool, before you get squashed or something,' yelled Dario La, adjusting one of his belts about his belly. Many hands reached out to Stave to help him up, and they hauled him out of the water pit, back onto the dry platform. The level of water began to decrease at a fast rate.

My clothes are dry.

Now, reverberating from the darkened tunnel, adding to the sound of slopping and hissing of sprayed liquid, came the noise of squealing and clanging; that of metal scraping over metal, and metal hitting upon metal; with a beat and a pulse and a pace.

'Whoever's dreaming this unknown terror deserves to be punished,' someone shouted and his words echoed down the underground train platform.

16 : SOLID RESCUE UNDERGROUND

'WHAT IS IT?' cried out a young woman. 'I'm getting really worried now.'

An air of oppressiveness and clamminess descended, no different than that felt with the onset of a storm.

'There isn't any need to panic everyone, keep calm. It might be a motorboat from the underground resources team with a crew. Some kind of rescue,' Stave answered to reassure them all. 'It could even be…' he paused, 'alright, I don't know what else it could be.'

Dario La called out over the heads of the others.

'Well, that's just dandy, isn't it? He doesn't know what it is.'

Stave was becoming annoyed.

'Fine, you tell us what it is, if you think you're so clever.'

'I never said I was clever. You said you were clever, in your clever green suit.'

'I don't recall saying anything of the sort. And my suit is turquoise.'

'Turquoise, lurkwoise, whatever. I'm insulted how you are interpreting my dream with the unknown. I was promised a gathering; I promised myself I'd get there. And I must find my bicycle.'

Feeling real in the unreal yet again, or unreal in the real; whichever it is, swinging from one extreme to the other, a giddy pendulum of emotions.

'Whether it be my dream or yours, it's still real enough,' Stave replied, 'so we've all got to pull ourselves together. It could be help on the way for us. I'll go and see.'

'So you can get to the gathering before me? Typical.'

'I never said that. I've no idea how to get to this gathering everyone keeps on talking about, if that satisfies you.'

'I'll tell you what will satisfy me—'

'Stop squabbling like babies in a pram,' shouted one of the waiting group. Now there were sounds of the hissing of pistons from inside the tunnel joined with the reverberated noises of splashing and grinding. 'Whatever it is, it's getting louder and sending waves down the stream. And the stream's getting lower, do you see? I think we ought to stand at the other end, to be on the safe side.'

'You can do that if you want but I'm going up to that tunnel entrance to see what's coming out,' Stave said and he marched with determination one way while the majority of the other passengers walked past him towards the other end, to collect there. They stood close to each other within a mauve shadow, looking like a single, dark block of stone. The trainee agent – the former bus driver – with the double rows of teeth, sat on the platform with his feet above the water. He pushed himself forward and once in, waded away from the noise. As he entered the tunnel at the far end, his shadow disintegrated into grey and blue snake-like shapes, and were taken away by the rippling flow of the stream over the tracks.

Stave stared intently at the left-hand tunnel mouth, to see the beginning of a magnificent metal horse emerge, at least twelve feet high from head to hoof, and fourteen feet long. Spurts of steam came from its nostrils. Its large head was formed from strips of deep brown iron. The mane was melded strands of alloy, on a thick neck. The huge plated body appeared, made with hexagons of bronze and copper, globules of mercury seeping from under the plates of the giant shoulders. There were spots of verdigris and rust in streaks over the mighty body panels. The artificial creature lifted its heavy hooves – shod with gunmetal – as if a show horse, above the lowering level of water. Each time a hoof descended, a shower of liquid shot from the surface. And as the incredible animal machine walked out further, it exposed exotic filigree chiseled onto its copper flanks, and a moulded tail made from fused, spun wire.

At the base of its thick, metal neck was an iron ring. Through the ring was a wide and stout pole. Attached to either end were long shafts connected to a gypsy caravan behind. Stave watched in awe as the mighty horse pulled the high caravan fully into view. The carved wheels of it were massive and they turned like watermill wheels.

The front of the caravan was painted in bright shades, the pictures and patterns on them raised as if enamelled. On the side were depictions of moons, suns, and stars as a border, and a life-size image of a jester within. This figure had green leaves woven into his blond hair, his head aimed upwards. There was an impression upon the face of deep thought or complete vacancy of mind, Stave couldn't decide. The jester wore a decorated tunic with an orange lining showing from the wide sleeves. In his right hand, held up over his shoulder, was a staff, with a red feather and a leather pouch tied to the end. In his left hand was a silver rose. Below the stockinged legs and booted feet – standing on a craggy ledge – was a prancing white dog. The background was vivid yellow, showing snow-tipped mountains and a stylized sun. As Stave walked over to it, the dog's head turned to him, silently panting with the strange terrier's toothy grin.

The image of the jester spoke quickly.

'You must follow your dream.'

Now the gigantic horse and caravan stood on the tracks, completely out of the tunnel. The trimming around the back door and the edges of the caravan was fretwork, showing delicately appreciated wooden coils and swirls.

Stave sat on the edge of the station platform and jumped into the water-filled rails. He waded over to the caravan and stepped up onto wooden steps at the back of it, then climbed onto a short stage. The metal horse, in all its glory, was perfectly still except for a nod of the massive head now and then, which gave the sound of screeching metal; and steam rose about it from its flared nostrils.

Stave knocked on the ornately-decorated caravan. There was no answer, so he opened the door and entered.

The interior, by contrast with the outside, was plain and empty except for a broom in one corner of the slat-lined walls. It caught his attention. He went to it and turned it vertically, so that the head was uppermost. The hairs on it were fine and they glistered. He scrutinized them with the magnifying glass, seeing that each bristle was a minuscule broom of its own. Then he quickly flipped the magnifying glass over to stop the broom from enlarging.

The sound of falling masonry from outside broke the silence of his introspection. Upon going out onto the caravan stage, he saw that the group of passengers who had collected together had become a crumbling stone block. Chunks were rolling and falling from it, and splintering when they hit the platform. Stave was startled. Only Dario La and one other stood there, alone on the grey platform.

'This is all of your doing,' Dario shouted over to Stave.

'How so?' Stave answered.

Dario La merely shrugged.

More falling masonry from the other end.

Stave couldn't bear to watch the destruction of the stone that had been people any longer. He rushed back inside.

17 : HELP FROM BEYOND THE REALM

HE WAS SURPRISED to find that the interior of the caravan was now lightly decorated with bunches of wildflowers and simple pottery figurines on the walls. And it was inhabited.

'Good evening, good morning, good afternoon,' an elderly woman said with sincerity and clarity, and she gave a sweet smile as if in recognition of Stave. She sat at a round table, a linen chequerboard tablecloth upon it. And placed upon this, in the centre, were four clear glass bells. On the woman's head was a hat of an unusual design. There were glass droplets about the banded and striped circumference. The woman looked tired but intelligent and amiable. She wore a full-length, purple skirt that glistened as it caught the light, with golden streaks appearing and disappearing, not unlike electricity sparks. And around her shoulders was a cape with a silver rose pinned to it. About her neck was a metal ring with a cowbell attached.

'Please, sit down,' she said and gestured to a simple wooden chair standing on the other side of the table.

'The passengers, they've crumbled,' Stave let out with concern. 'Outside, on the station platform. Take a look.'

The woman's worn expression changed to curiosity, her

saddened eyes sparkling.

A lucid beauty of mind emanating from behind that old face. So familiar and yet, now, not…

'Do you really believe that those people crumbled if they were real?' she asked, placing her head to one side and then the other, the glass ornaments about her hat tinkling, and gleaming as though lit from the inside. Her artistic-looking hands, faceted as if made from marble, were held above the table. Her long fingers moved slowly like a sea anemone being wafted by currents, or as if she played gentle notes on a piano, invisible to the eye. 'The mistakes due to your lack of memory and naivety are charming. But please, see for yourself,' she added and, after placing her palms together as if an act of prayer, she let them drift apart again. A small concertina appeared. She moved the bellows with slow, silent claps. The instrument produced wistful musical sighs and atmospheric, bowed string vibrations.

Stave looked out of the door; the group of people was restored.

'How can this be?'

'You are constantly forgetting and lost, not understanding the reality of the situation. Blame some of that onto the dream winds. Some of the people you have met, or will meet, aren't real. They are mere dream elements – dream cast, as you might have heard.'

'Yes, dream cast, I remember again now. And I do swing from being lost in a dream to being lost in a reality like a dream.'

'All part of Tremelon Zandar's doing,' the woman said. 'Wait a moment,' – the clear sound of one of the bells on the table – 'Now how do you see the dream cast?'

Stave went out onto the stage of the caravan and called back.

'Pink flamingos on the platform, each of them standing on one leg. Though I see Dario La and another still there, arguing.'

'Then those arguing are as real as you and I,' the old lady explained. 'Please, come back inside.' Stave did as she asked. She continued, 'You don't recognise me at all, do you?' and she looked almost sad.

'Should I?' Stave queried.

A peculiar sense of belonging; spiritual comfort, longing.

'Eventually, I can look like anyone I wish again. At the moment you see me as an ageing person. We have been apart for too long. I have missed you so much.'

'I'm not certain I know what you are talking about. Madam, you are a stranger to me and old enough to be my mother. Then that's who you are, my mother?'

The woman let out a delightful laugh tinged with sadness.

'Oh, if only I could tell you the whole story! Tremelon Zandar has erased your memory again as I'm sure you have come to realise. But once we have defeated him and his army of agents then you will understand, and begin to remember. Learn again too.'

Stave sat and looked into her bright eyes, deep and full of wisdom.

You have the most incredible eyes I have ever seen.

Thank you, that's lovely of you to say, Stave heard in his head.

'So you can hear my thoughts as well?'

'Only if you want. But you've lost the ability to shut your

mind to others, along with the loss of many other abilities.'

'Abilities, like what?'

'The more I tell, the more there's the danger we are being overheard, the less I must say.'

'Heard by Tremelon Zandar?' Stave asked.

'Yes. He may have overtaken but there are still many secrets hidden from him. He must never know the full story or we are all lost.'

'I expect he knows because of the cowbells around our necks.'

'Partly, yes,' she replied.

'And marking with rosettes.'

'Oh, I didn't know that. He has multiple ways of marking people, that much I do know. He tries to be creative.'

'Yes, two people I met on the bus – Mariella and Quikso – were given them. Now they can't take them off.'

'You know them well, Stave. Another mind blank has made you forget.'

'That's not surprising. I thought they seemed familiar. I hope they are safe.'

'When did you last see them?'

'Quikso Lebum on the bus and Mariella Fortana on the underground train.'

The old woman shut her eyes and appeared to be concentrating. When they opened again, she pointed to the back of the caravan where the slats were decorated with the hanging dried flowers and clay figurines. Amongst them, a wine bottle stuck out at right angles, its base firmly fixed to the wood of the wall.

'Maybe that dream-summoned item will help in finding

one or both of them,' she said.

A gentle pulsation of light came from within the bottle. Stave skirted the table and went to it, looking through the open end as if it were a telescope. He saw, tinted green by the bottle glass, the interior of an underground train carriage, with Mariella Fortana seated, contentedly inspecting one of her wooden fish.

'So, Mariella is safe. That's good news,' he said and walked over the floorboards to the front of the table. 'I hope Quikso is safe too. Tell me, are you a magician or a type of sorceress, or perhaps even a gypsy who can foretell the future with the aid of a crystal ball or similar?'

As the woman rubbed her palms together, the concertina was no more. She smiled pleasantly.

'None of those things. Though a sorceress of sorts, able to amplify and modify frequencies of energy. I will endeavour to explain more of that later. Enough to say, most of my abilities have been taken away, like yours, Stave Swirler, so at the moment I am no more than a stage conjuror.'

'I don't know how you know my name, but that is correct. May I ask your name?'

She picked up a bell and a cloud of moths flew from it to the ceiling.

'I am Cassaldra Chimewood. One of my many names. We met a long time ago.'

Cassaldra Chimewood: that name rings truth and destiny, happiness even. But why? A subtle remembrance of … now gone. I have a gaping wound in my mind that needs to be filled with positive certainty. For some reason, I feel I want to hug her.

'I'm pleased to meet you, madam. So we've met before?'

'That is so sweet that you say madam. Please call me Cassaldra, like you've always done. And yes, we have met many times.'

Stave went to the side of the table and held out a hand in greeting but flames appeared, made of red crêpe paper, though they were as hot as any real fire.

'Why did you do that?' he asked, offended. 'I wouldn't have harmed you, I only wished to shake your hand.'

'Please understand, I know that. This is the doing of Tremelon Zandar. He has me trapped in a dream cage which I am unable to escape from. Sit and gently lean forward.'

Stave returned to the front of the table and did as he was asked. He was confronted with more paper flames emanating heat. And beyond, he viewed Cassaldra sitting in a cage, set in a courtyard with its stone walls streaked with iron bars. Upon leaning back in his chair, Cassaldra Chimewood was in the caravan again.

'I understand, of sorts,' He said. 'It seems Tremelon and his agents have many abilities, to trap people, turning agents' hands to crab-like claws…'

'And worse,' Cassaldra said. 'He has stolen abilities more powerful than you know at the moment.'

'Have you known Tremelon Zandar for long?'

'Nowhere as long as I've known you.'

'Yet I've no memory of ever meeting you before. Then what can you tell me about my past?'

'I could tell you much about your past but that will be for another time. You must first come to terms with the present, try to understand what has been happening, and why. Don't be upset or perturbed. There are explanations if you are prepared to listen. And I am ready to tell you the truth again, providing you keep calm. We must speak quietly and quickly.' The old lady placed her two thumbs together and Stave smelled a heady scent of rose petals. 'But first I will pose some questions, if you have no objections.' Stave shook his head and then she said, 'Where are you?'

What a peculiar thing to ask.

'I'm here, talking to you in a gypsy caravan,' Stave replied. Cassaldra's eyebrows raised to promote more. 'The caravan is pulled by an amazing horse made of different types of metal. It's standing on an underground railway track which has become flooded.'

'Is there anything unusual in what you have just said?'

With another shake of the head, Stave replied, 'Why should there be? It all is out of the ordinary but I've grasped the fact that I'm dreaming in reality. At least, I think I am.'

'Good, you've worked that out for yourself,' Cassaldra said. 'Can you remember how you got here?'

'I only remember a time from being on a bus, journeying through a tunnel, no more of my past. Except that perhaps I live in a cottage on the edge of the woods. And I might have been going shopping at the Olympian Shopping Mall. Or heading for the gathering? A lot of people I've met seem to be going there.'

'You are trapped in a dream loop. But let us take things step by step. It will take time, because of your memories having been erased, as Tremelon Zandar tries to do with me—'

Stave said, 'I'm sorry to hear that. As for me, it seems he and his agents want my guts for guitar strings, to put a no finer point on it.' His eyes were hunting about the caravan interior as if in fear of the enemy appearing from nowhere. Then there was a chime from a mantlepiece clock standing on a pillar by the door. Stave seemed to become calmer upon hearing it.

Cassaldra drew in a breath.

'After I have explained more, you will ask many questions, which I will try to answer, if we have time. Before that, I will give you an explanation for the appearance of the clock. It was there for me. I thought it into actual existence. It's called dream summoning. This is one of my abilities I have left.'

'Yes, I have had experience of that already. I summoned hooks onto Mariella's wooden fish, and a snorkel to breathe underwater.'

'Ah, that is good. Obviously your experience and power with dream summoning hasn't totally been taken away.'

Cassaldra stood. And while concentrating once again, the clock vanished, then appeared upon the table before her. She gracefully sat once more.

'So, in this caravan we are all in your dream in reality?' Stave said.

'Yes and no. If only I could start at the beginning, but there is no one beginning. And even if there were, I'm certain I wouldn't always remember.' She sighed. 'The majority of what you see here at the moment is part of my dream, my lucid dream which I have created in reality. The rest is yours, as well as other people. I am not dreaming you nor are you dreaming me. We are dreamers together. We are all dreamers in the one dream reality.' There was silence other than a clank of metal from the horse outside. Cassaldra paused and took a deep breath before continuing, 'I will tell you this much: there is an old man – much older than you can imagine – a remarkable man of wisdom and honour, a man of courage and love, who can be fully conscious within his dreams. But there's more. He has been given a dream realm, where he can overlay dream elements onto reality while he is awake – I'm talking about lucid dreaming within all that is real.'

'Lucid dreams?'

'You have even been made to forget that? When we are dreaming normally, we are not aware of being asleep or of being in a dream-state. But there is a higher state, to be fully aware within reverie, to feel more real even than in an awakened state. That is lucid dreaming. The elements, choices, and decisions within the dream can be made as though consciously. Anything you desire can be.'

'So this is a lucid dream, albeit shared,' Stave said.

'More even than a lucid dream. You were correct to say a dream within reality. This man I speak of was the first ever to be bestowed a wonder, a unique place, an extraordinary visionary world created within the labyrinths of his mind, whilst sleeping or awake; creating remarkable places within lucid dreams but also in reality. To explain further, this world is a separate existence, a parallel universe – the melding of reality as we know it through our faculties, with the infinite universe of lucid dreams. He then passed on this discovered door and key.'

'A real door and key?'

'I'm speaking in the spiritual sense. The door would be a turning point, a particular way to enter his complex mind, his remarkable realm. The key is to unlock understanding, enlightenment, a culmination of wisdom, empowerment of mind within. And once through the door, to be able to experience the parallel universe without the necessity of being asleep. And for others to learn the progression.'

Stave was becoming intrigued by what he was listening to, although he was uncertain as to whether or not he fully understood her words.

He realised all at once he had left his chair and had been pacing up and down the floorboards of the caravan. He sat again.

'A progression to what, may I ask?'

'A progression to a goal. And the goal?' Cassaldra gently opened the back of the antique clock, carefully taking out the workings from the casing and placing them on the table. 'This is exquisite workmanship, do you not agree? It is lovely to see each cog and wheel, each part dependent on each other, every element painted in matching hues with such precision, to match the precise workings of the mechanism. The goal is one's own state of being where the physicality of self is totally united with the emotional, spiritual conscious evocations within the mind. Space and time no longer need to have firm delineation; no boundaries or limitations. This is all as it was until this special reality was infiltrated by Tremelon Zandar.'

Stave felt as if, under his turquoise suit, he was made of glass.

An unusual sensation.

He vigorously nodded. This was making sense in some fundamental way although he was becoming overwhelmed.

'It's all too much to take on board at once but I think I

understand. So basically you are saying that the old man you spoke of has been given the ability to be fully awake but still can have dreams at the same time.'

'That is correct. As can others who are invited. It's a difficult concept to comprehend, I know. Your physical, mental, and spiritual body is here, with me; you touch the chair and table as solid, as real. And yet I can do this.' She held out her purple sleeves. She placed her wrists together, and formed a bowl shape with her fingers. The bells in the clock began to play, the clappers clearly swinging. And about them, a ring of bright moths flew in a circular flight path. 'Here is a simple dream element in reality.'

'I see. But one aspect I don't understand here, Cassaldra. Why would anyone want the reality of pain within a dream?'

'Anything to do with pain given, or the reasons our bodies give pain, should not be a part of our realm,' she replied. 'Only everyday pleasure – the touch of texture and form, the smell of a flower, the hearing of mysterious music, the sight of everyday wonders, these should be felt and experienced. Peace, love, and happiness for those peace-loving kind. The feeling of shaking the hand of another, or of a kiss, making love, or an embrace; these things can be felt. Any pain, any act which would cause pain or any sort of suffering, whether mental or physical, any aggression or attack, is from a small but powerful set only, led by one person: Tremelon Zandar.'

'The one and the same who is after me. Who is after you too?'

'He is no longer after me.'

'Why is that?'

'Because he has already captured me.'

'Could I ask, this special man you mentioned, can't he help?' Stave said.

'He's trying his best. He's learned a lot today.'

'Who is he? And how do you know so much about him?'

'One of his names is Marcello Sanctifus,' said Cassaldra. 'And he's my husband. That's all I can say at the moment.'

She stared hard into Stave's eyes as though expecting some reaction.

Stave merely nodded and said, 'But if you say I've known you for a long time but now forgotten, is that the same for your husband?'

The cowbell about Clarianne's neck began to rattle and she looked sad again.

'If only I could tell you – I've explained enough already – Tremelon could hear whatever else I wish to explain to you, so I must say no more on that point.'

'Can't you take off the cowbell?'

'My fingers would drop from my palms with frostbite before I managed to move it an inch,' she replied. 'The same with you, as you've probably discovered.'

Stave agreed.

I must find this Tremelon Zandar and stop him.

Shafts of light within the cabin seemed to vibrate as the gypsy caravan shook. Cassaldra lowered her voice.

'Tremelon Zandar is different for each person. If we are a group of people within a reality dreamscape, individuals as caretakers and patrons and guests, Tremelon Zandar is a conglomerate, an ill-blended concoction of many. He has stolen the key to the door which lies between everyday reality and our lucid dreams.'

Stave was curious.

'And so, if you and your husband are caretakers of lucid dreams within reality, then what is Tremelon Zandar the caretaker of?'

Cassaldra sighed, not with impatience but with sadness.

'Isn't it obvious? He is the caretaker of nightmares.'

18 : LOVE LOST TO A MIND CAGE

STAVE STOOD QUICKLY, holding his forehead with a palm.

'This is extraordinary yet it makes sense.'

'Indeed it does,' Cassaldra Chimewood answered. She appeared to be made of shimmering light. 'We must fight back with the meagre talents we have left.'

'Does that mean we all are appearing in Tremelon's nightmare?' he asked with growing apprehension.

'Not at the moment. But he is using cunning and subtle ways to alter our dream reality.'

Stave noticed that the chair which he had been sitting on was no longer there and that the seated Cassaldra, and the table before her, were now at the side wall of the caravan cabin. There was even a bare part of the wall at the back, the dried flowers and figurines having apparently moved over nearer to a corner. The four bells upon the table had melted together.

'Is there some significance to the fact that you have moved since I first met you here, Cassaldra?' he asked, puzzled.

'Combined lucid dreams, created by many dreamers, have laws, not unlike the laws of nature. Positive elements within our dream could be created by anyone who has the necessary experience. It would seem that I am, for want of a better explanation, at the end of a transparent pendulum which has started moving again. I will bid you farewell now, for I will be gone soon enough.'

'Will we be meeting again?'

'I truely hope so. There are many lucid dream realms but all are contained within one sphere, invaded by the agents of Tremelon Zandar. We must become powerful enough to banish him and his followers.'

The table was vanishing into the wall of the caravan as if being eaten. Already Cassaldra's caped shoulder and right arm were no longer visible, apparently dissolved by the wooden side of the caravan.

'Goodbye for now, Stave Swirler, and remember I love you.'

Love me? Do I love you? Perhaps you are a relative...I feel a strange loss, now that you're going.

'You will know the full truth one day,' she said as she disappeared through the caravan wall.

Stave walked hurriedly out again to the stage, peering down the side of the caravan. Cassaldra Chimewood was nowhere to be seen.

The water outside had flowed away. Without warning, the metal horse quivered and jolted into motion, lurching forward, the clopping of hooves sounding like echoed, distant claps of thunder, with the caravan cabin creaking and swaying while being pulled.

He moved to the other side of the stage and called over to Dario La, who now stood alone on the station platform.

'Quickly, Dario, join me here. It could be the way out.'

'I'll take my chances and wait for another train,' Dario La replied, his voice reverberating.

'But that's unlikely soon, isn't it. Come on.'

'You go on your own, in your dapper turquoise suit. If there's not another train, I'm bound to find a way out. The flamingos are concentrated in a flock by a metal gate that's appeared. Worth investigating.' He pulled his trousers higher up over his generous stomach by pulling on his two belts.

'OK, if you insist,' Stave answered.

He watched Dario La stride over to his companion who was already by the gate.

'It's unlocked,' Dario shouted back, the flock of flamingos strutting about him. 'You coming along?'

'No, I'm going to see where this horse takes me. Thanks, all the same. I hope you get to the gathering. And find your bicycle.'

'Cheers, snazzy man. There are stairs the other side; they've got to lead somewhere.'

Stave waved to Dario La.

'Good luck,' he said as the tunnel swallowed him, the horse and the caravan.

19 : INDICATIONS OF DREAMS ABANDONED

EITHER SIDE OF the dimly lit tunnel hung lengths of knotted rope, the light coming from pale yellow lamps. The rails of the tracks were no more, and in their place were damp paving stones set amidst gravel. There was clanking and hissing of the great metal horse, the rumbling of wheels, and creaking of the caravan, as it made its way along that grimy tunnel.

How familiar Cassaldra seemed. How could I forget I know her, yet still feel I know her? Even the metal horse and caravan ring bells in my mind as I travel this dismal tunnel. I'll sit on the floorboards as we lurch forward and wait to find out my final destination. The Olympian Shopping Mall? I'll be patient. I can do nothing else but wait.

After a while, Stave walked out onto the stage and looked down the length of the caravan to check on progress as they moved steadily along. He passed mannequins behind glass, set into the walls, and strange machines made of copper and brass.

There was an alcove in the dark tunnel wall with a crow within it, pecking at a starfish. And as it did so, the sea creature squealed as if a kitten in torment. The baleful bird paused in its task to turn its head to Stave, and he saw it had musty blue pins for eyes.

Further on, a sizeable hole in the side of the tunnel came into view. Beyond stood a beautiful hill scattered with radiant flowers, and bushes made of silk with birds dotted amongst them. Dragonflies, the size of canines, zipped here and there with their glorious iridescent bodies, translucent wings humming. At the top of the hill stood an impressive castle with lofty turrets bathed in bright sunlight, the pleasant solitude punctured only by the bird calls.

Stave climbed down off the caravan's stage, through the hole, and went to the beginning of the hill. But the further towards it he walked, the further away it seemed to be. That was until he broke into a run and clambered up the steep slope. The hill had become no more than artificial turf on a small pile. At the top, the silk bushes were piles of coal, and the castle merely a toy made of wooden bricks. The large dragonflies lay on the mock grass, now made of twitching plastic. Sounds of birds had become the noise of wood being scratched.

Disappointed, Stave turned away and walked back onto the caravan stage. He sat with his legs over the edge as the caravan rumbled on, hissing and whooshing still emanating from the massive metal beast pulling it along.

They travelled through what once might have been an impressive orangery containing exotic plants and shrubs, and trees with colourful blossom. But now all were dying and decaying; now only dead leaves and dried stems on shrivelled trees, and weeds in their crumbling containers could be seen. Smashed and smeared windows let through a dull, grey light and howling moans of a wind. Puffs of flying insects and grey smoke hung in the stifling and polluted air.

Between the decay littering the paving stones of the floor were sleeping blue snakes, and piles of copper pipes, their surface turned to verdigris. A solemn ambience hung over the orangery and Stave was glad to be reaching its end to enter the tunnel again.

Through another break in the tunnel wall, he saw a mansion house. It was an imposing structure, even with its frontage ripped away, and scaffolding holding up the sides. The interiors of the panelled rooms were empty, antique furniture, the carpets and chandeliers having been piled unceremoniously on the orange gravelled frontage. A sea rolled in with dark blue waves that crashed into the ground floor rooms before receding. Blue worms were left behind and they wriggled away into corners.

As if emotion can seep into a structure and be released to the viewer, the whole scene emanated sadness, forlornness even. The roaring sea rolled in again and completely covered the mansion with a wave that looked like a giant hand.

The caravan continued forward in the darkened tunnel with the rumbling of wheels, and hissing and clopping of the mighty metal horse. There were flitting shadows of bats.

The horse machine and caravan came upon a fork in the tunnel. The horse seemed to know instinctively which direction to take. One tunnel leading off to the left appeared shrouded in gloom, while the other was lit from no apparent source of lighting, a soft haze pervading its length. Upon continuing along this lighted section, Stave had a sense of anticipation come upon him. Peering ahead, he could make out rippling water.

20 : CORAL CAVE OF THE MINDS

As THE METAL horse neared the end of the tunnel, a still pool within a chamber of rock could be seen laying ahead – no less than a circular cavern. The horse lumbered on and descended into the clear water. It bowed its head, enough to tap the surface, sending more ripples to the edges. There was a peaceful and restful atmosphere, cool and quiet. High up in a vaulted ceiling were cracked and chipped frescos within squares of sculpted stone edging. They showed figures that moved in slow pantomime within bright landscapes.

Jutting out from the rough limestone walls – the texture like dripped and dried resin – were tapering stone pillars, surrounded by stalagmites and stalactites of green crystal.

On the rippling pond were large brain-like corals, the size of cars, drifting slowly. And below the surface, small fish darted. A group of jellyfish wafting in shoals, all moving like a flock of birds would. They were like gelatine bowler hats with tassels and streamers. Stave crouched on the caravan stage and leaned over to inspect them further, and upon an impulse, scooped one out. It had the texture of a wet pillowcase and it disintegrated between his fingers as if it had been made of clear icing sugar.

He sat down on the wooden planks of the stage and saw flitting flecks of light and shadow, dappling and streaking the walls.

He watched with interest as two of the corals gently moved together, becoming one larger coral, before splitting into three or four smaller ones. The interaction of the floating corals were acting like bubbles, constantly joining and splitting off again. Gentle, echoed popping sounds came from them.

Contentment. The first time for hours. Or days or months, for all I know. Nothing to do now but sit and contemplate as I gaze at the fish under the shimmering surface of the cavern pool. Even the metal horse has become still. A humming of delicate air; most soothing.

After a while, he spotted a long crack in one of the walls with a shaft of light splaying from it, highlighting motes and specks in the cavern air. Stave slipped into the water and waded towards it. He was feeling adventurous and he smiled all at once, untroubled within his contentment, even though his passage through the water felt as if he moved through treacle.

The closer he got to the crack, the louder he could hear mechanical groans and whines, powerful engines and metallic crashes. When he put an eye to the split rock, clouds of dust and smoke obscured his vision to a muddy area, lit with halogen lights on aluminium poles. As the dust cleared, Stave could clearly see some of the bulbs on the poles were smashed, and work cabins flattened. Two tractors were on the mud, the bucket grabs of the powerful machines held up, the engines roaring as if bellowing at each other. Slate tiles, bricks, and other debris lay scattered across the churned mud. The tractor engines became silent. Way beyond the tractors stood a tall building cut from a grey sky, marked "Olympian Shopping Mall", the top of it ringed with grey haloes. Blue flames came from its many windows.

The engine of one of the tractors roared into life once more, the caterpillar tracks crushing bricks and blocks. Its grab bucket was raised then lowered swiftly to collide with the bucket of the other. Both drivers wore plain, featureless masks. They frenziedly wrenched and jerked the stick controls. A yellow dumper truck and a small lorry appeared from out of the smokey haze and rammed them both with the sounds of crushing metal and engines screeching. The tractor picked up a mash of builders' materials, attempting to offload it onto the driver's cab of the lorry. The other tractor's occupant was aiming the toothy grab to fall onto the dumper truck. Within the din and dust and mayhem, workers were running at each other, scuffling and throwing hard hats; some were hitting out with lengths of planed wood or metal bars.

Stave took his head away, back into the quietness of the cavern with the pinheads of silver winking on the pool. Whatever was happening there, with those agents of Tremelon within the underground construction site, he wanted nothing to do with it.

The treacle water was thickening more, feeling and looking like quicksand; he found he was unable to move his legs. He was up to his waist in the orange grains, small pads of water collecting in depressions on top. He took off his turquoise jacket and placed it onto the sand, laying over it.

He moved forward on his chest, extricating his legs from the suction that the sodden sand made. Once out, he retrieved the jacket and trod over the surface, already solidifying, back to the half-buried caravan, and the metal horse with its flared nostrils touching the sand drifts, trapped within it up to its back. The spun wire tail fell and rose, a spray of sand flying, as if it were trying to dig itself out.

The large coral hemispheres were alive with pink crabs and swarms of midges.

Stave walked onto the planked stage and entered the caravan again. There were piles of sand on the floor with cogs and starfish scattered over them, and the heady perfume of jasmine in the air. He found two small metal feathers sticking from the yellow sand and took them.

At the back, there was now the outline of a door. Around it were the shapes of eye masks, inlaid with marquetry. In place of a door handle was a deep slot. Hanging above the door was a proper eye mask with colourful swirls upon it. He took it and placed it on his head, over his eyes.

He pushed upon the door. There was no movement.

Dream logic was required, he considered. He retrieved Quikso Lebum's business card – which had been punched by the ticket inspector on the underground train – and placed it into the slot.

Immediately after, the door clicked and swung slowly open.

21 : GATHERING OF THE COMBINED DREAM

'MR QUIKSO LEBUM, again to the gathering,' announced a tall man, dressed in the finest of silk shirts and tie, slick black trousers and smart tailed jacket, with his deep baritone voice projected over the assembled guests. They stood with filled glasses in their hands, each wearing an eye mask of a different design. All heads were turned to Stave and they gave loud, undisguised laughs, some toasting him by lifting their glasses to the air. Then they continued their discourse upon a perfect square of grass, bounded by tall hedges, immaculately pruned. Along the tops, exquisite topiary could be seen, showing lines of running hares. The night sky was a deep, bottle green, points of light blinking, slowly moving in endless patterns. Distant voices like the whisper of a faraway sea.

Stave was taken aback.

'I'm not Quikso Lebum, I'm Stave Swirler,' he said from the corner of his mouth in a low voice.

This much I know. And I own a cottage at the edge of the woods. And I'm lost in dream reality.

'Not Mr Quikso Lebum but the honourable Mr Stave Swirler once more,' bellowed the announcer. Then, turning to Stave, he added in a quieter voice, 'Was that acceptable?'

A little cloud drifted past his finger and he twirled it as if it were white candy floss, or thick, compliant smoke.

Stave shrugged.

'I suppose it is. Thank you for the fine introduction. I'm guessing Quikso Lebum is already here. But why did you introduce me with the words "once more"?'

'Why, Mr Swirler, this must be your sixth or seventh visit. You mention that every time.'

'How preposterous.' *Or is it? I am suffering from a serious loss of memory, after all. And Cassaldra did say I've been put into a time loop.* 'Enough to tell you, I wasn't expecting to come to this place nor do I remember being here before. And I don't know anyone here. Nor does anyone knows me, I suspect. Except for Quikso.'

'You say that every time as well,' the announcer said and he laughed while brushing silver dust from his jacket.

The sound of humming violins.

'Hmm, Whatever I say, I've said exactly the same, those times before? So, let it be.' He swept his sight over the night scene. 'It doesn't seem much of a gathering. I expected hundreds of people here. What sort of gathering is it?'

'Not as many people have found the gathering this time around. And the answer to what sort of gathering this is, it's for those assembled to be given the greatest adventure ever known. That is unless Tremelon Zandar spoils things yet again.'

'I've have experienced enough of him and his agents already,' Stave replied. 'Let us hope not. Anyway, what should I do, mingle?'

'What do you want to do? Mingle if you wish; stand, walk, don't walk, sit, take in the warm night atmosphere perhaps; partake of wine or ale. Be smothered in a delightful scent of flowers maybe.'

Once that was said, with the gentle music pervading the air, roses and carnations fell from nowhere to the perfect grass. The stars were sending down streaks of light which played over the dancing guests dressed in black suits and ballroom gowns. Every time a spot of light passed Stave's nose there was a delicate aroma. But when the light had passed, he smelled mouldering mushrooms.

'I'm not sure about the odour of decaying fungi,' Stave said.

'That,' the announcer replied, 'would be emanating from the cowbell about your neck, sir. I'd try to avoid it as best you can.'

'Not possible. It's made of a sort of metal that seems welded to me in some mystical fashion. It worries me; Cassaldra Chimewood tells me there's no way of getting rid of the awful thing.'

Stave looked down his aquiline nose to it.

'Ah, you've met Cassaldra again, excellent. As I must tell you every time, you are indeed honoured, sir. A wonderful woman. If that is what she says, then that is so.'

'Have you been here long, at the gathering?'

The man gave a becoming smile.

'For a few months or more, on and off. At least I think it's been that long. Or was it yesterday or the day before? Time is meaningless in a way, where we are.'

Stave raised his eyebrows.

'That long in a reality dream? That's presuming you know you are dreaming within the wakeful real.'

His attention was drawn away for a moment by the topiary hares loping across the tops of the bushes for a few seconds, and flashes of yellow and red lightning illuminating distant hills. Through a wide gap in one of the hedges could be seen the still waters of a dark lake. The occasional fish would leap from out of it, and where the circular ripples reached the edge of the lake, magenta sparks flew and sparkled with the sounds of tinkling bells.

The man said, 'Yes, I do know I am dreaming. Not that everyone here does. Those would be the invited dreamers within a lucid dreamers' realm. Not counting the others.'

'You mean the dream cast? Dreams of the dreamers.'

'Yes, dreams of the dreamers; while a few could be agents of Tremelon.'

'We should all go back,' Stave said. 'That way, they can't affect anyone.'

There was a slight breeze within the pleasant warmth of the night.

The announcer became serious.

'Go back where? And even if we knew where, we can't,' he said, shrugging. 'Many of us have been here for a long time. We are all trapped, waiting for Marcello Sanctifus to show us the way.'

'And what will happen when he shows you the way?'

'Sir, miracles will happen.'

As the announcer's sight flicked to Stave's cowbell again, there were smiles and light laughter from the parading and twirling guests on the grass. Winding between their legs was a miniature steam train, the size of a greyhound. A mechanical device on the front fetched track lines from thin air, laying them before it as it went. Yellow smoke came from its chimney, forming into cubes and spheres before disappearing into the night air. The train pulled a small coach and as it approached any dancing couple, it deftly changed direction to avoid a collision. It twisted and turned, chugging around them and between them. The tracks behind the carriage were picked up by another mechanical hand and placed into the top of it. The train appeared as playful as any young canine; indeed, some were beckoning it and patting their knees.

I could do with a drink. And I don't give permission for my thoughts to be heard.

'You want a drink,' the announcer stated and a glass of red wine appeared, balancing on his upturned palm. Then with his hand extending from a white sleeve with cufflinks showing, he gave Stave the glass.

'Did you read my mind as well? How annoying.'

'Shouldn't be annoying at all. Here in the gathering, there is a form of collective consciousness even though we retain our individuality. You'll get used to it. It is a difficult concept to grasp and many don't bother to anyway. Whether or not you understand the principles of the realms is not important.'

'But I didn't give you permission.'

'I see what you mean. That is true: choice has been taken away here. That'll be more nefarious meddling by the evil ones. Sometimes it works to block your thoughts if you wish, other times it doesn't.'

'What if I thought a bad thing?' Stave asked, as the little

train raced up to him, immediately placing a curved piece of track before it and rolling around him. 'I could decide that the small, black train was an angry, venomous snake, for instance.'

'All goodly guests here have no conscious desire to hurt anyone, you included. You wouldn't harm anyone in reality nor will you be able to here. Apart from that, very few people have the ability to amend the dream reality. That is one of the gifts which we will be taught by Marcello Sanctifus. See for yourself – think something bad and there will be no effect.'

The train will transform into a ten feet long cobra, spitting acid.

Immediately, the train became an extended, coiling snake made of green felt, some of the cotton wool stuffing showing from splits along its length. As it wound about the delighted people, it would occasionally rise up as if about to strike and cough a cotton ball from its roughly sewn mouth. There was light applause.

'I am truly impressed,' the announcer said. 'Dream summoning at its best. How did you do that without being taught?'

'I don't know, but I've had a small amount of practice,' Stave replied.

'Excellent. That ability will see you in good stead for the future. So you see, you cannot cause problems. Even Tremelon has trouble causing trouble. He has to devise ways of leading people away.'

'To their nightmare, I know; I've learned that one.'

The lilting music stopped. Now could be heard a steady

beat, emanating from an entrance to a marquee. This was set in another perfect square of grass, seen through an opening of one of the hedges.

Stave continued, 'Well, he won't get me. And as much as I like it here at the gathering, I'll find a way back to true non-dream reality.'

'I don't know how you propose to do that. No one has succeeded for a long while. I'm not sure what you consider to be reality anyway,' the announcer replied. A woman with a coiled bun of hair came up to him and fluttered her eyelashes through her eye mask. 'Ah, the delightful Alicia. Now if you will excuse me, I wish to dance,' he said with a slight bow.

'Of course,' Stave replied but already the pair were twirling and parading over the evenly-lit grass, in front of the small lake reflecting the stars. Other couples were matching their movements and gestures. With waves of the hand, sparkling tinsel twisted in the air. With just the drumbeat emanating from the marquee, it became a ritualistic affair, as if they were attempting to pluck metaphysical truths from the night sky.

Stave took a few sips of his wine, placed the glass onto a white table, and walked nearer to the marquee entrance. The beat became stronger. Two people came out of the entrance, running towards him, their bodies jolting to the rhythm as if the sound was a physical object pounding the pair.

Stave immediately recognised them.

'Hi, remember me?' he said to the youth with the dark hair fringe across one eye and the studded dog collar about his neck.

'Sure I do,' Quikso Lebum replied. 'Going well? I thought

you were shopping. And here is Mariella,' and he nodded towards the young woman.

Mariella glared and said with an annoyed tone, 'Don't introduce me, we've already met several times.'

The muscles in her thin calf muscles were taught as if she was ready to spring away at any moment. Yet she seemed to lean closer to Quikso, as though she had something to hide behind his back.

Stave looked to Quikso for some clue as to why Mariella would not want to be introduced again. After all, he had helped her with the hooks for her wooden fish. He did, however, leave her on the underground train. Quikso picked up on the querulous expression upon Stave's face.

'It's not you, it's me upsetting her. We seem to have a hand problem – we're holding hands and Mariella doesn't like it.'

'Well, release hands then,' Stave suggested, as obvious as it was. He looked to Mariella's unblemished face with the dark mascara and painted lips. 'Glad you found your way to the gathering from the underground train.'

With the slim, free hand she stroked her once mahogany then blonde hair, now turned black, as if to comfort herself. And then, with tears springing from her distraught eyes, she ran, seemingly pulling Quikso away with her with the other hand, while he shouted out, 'You don't understand, Stave Swirler.'

The dancing couples had transformed into swaying trees, their exposed roots tapping at the leaf-strewn grass. Regular openings appeared down each trunk as if they could be some musical instrument, like an oboe or clarinet. Indeed, as waves of white and yellow silk sheets appeared from out of the openings, strange flute sounds frosted the air.

The silk sheets spun and spiralled in a beautiful dance.

A ballet of primal wraiths.

As those sheets moved, combining and parting about each other, all the while interacting with precision, they changed hues within mirage patterns about them.

Some of the gathering guests clapped their hands together while others laughed with delight at this dream episode.

A few of the animated silk sheets dropped to the superb lawn. And as they faded to nothing, Stave saw tiny objects on the emerald grass: three more miniature feathers.

He picked them up and put them into a pocket of his turquoise trousers with the others.

My unusual collection is coming on well.

Just as the dancing silk sheets remaining in the air began to combine in kaleidoscopic patterns, there was panic within the gathering guests. The cowbell around Stave's neck tightened and played with its clanging tone, giving off the smell of rotting mushrooms.

22 : REFLECTIONS OF EVIL DISGUISED

'AGENTS OF TREMELON close; beware, everyone,' someone shrieked.

The lake had become the sky, the sky now the shimmering lake. This watery glassy ceiling mirrored the gathering guests and the cloudy lawn. Billowing blooms of blue smoke above were descending from it, smelling of rust.

Don't look up. Another evil venture by Tremelon Zandar.

Those that did look up with fascination to the sky water, now choppy as if sea waves blown by a strong wind, saw their own reflections staring back at them – except for their masks. No longer eye masks upon them in the reflections, but full masks. Their visages upon them were at rest and emotionless, eyes closed, as if made from plaster that had been cast over their sleeping faces. The assembled few not looking upwards gazed with fascination at being able to walk through night clouds.

'You've all got to get out,' Stave shouted out to the guests and he ran from one still figure to another, attempting to bring their heads down.

The topiary hares loped fast amongst the crowd and through the ground clouds as though in fright.

Quikso wove his way between those seemingly hypnotised standing guests, with Mariella close behind him.

As smoke serpents were dropping to the grass from out of the lake water above that had turned ink blue, Mariella's shrill voice was heard above a sudden humming breeze, 'Leave me alone!'

Yet she still held hands with Quikso as she pulled him back towards the gap in the hedge, over to the entrance of the marquee.

Why doesn't she simply unlink hands? Peculiar behaviour.

Stave returned his attention to the entranced guests with their sights locked to the sky lake.

'Escape while you can!' he shouted to those guests milling aimlessly about through the clouds, while pulling at the frozen ones.

Stave decided to go after Quikso and Mariella.

'Quickly, follow me,' he bellowed to those guests still open to his suggestion.

He too went through the gap in the hedge, across a red carpet strewn with flowers, and then headed for the canvas marquee.

23 : ACROBATS AND STRANGERS

INSIDE THE MARQUEE was a vast arena. Many people strolled about, mingling and dispersing over the squares of grass that were painted with geometric designs. The powerful beat of the drum still throbbed like a heartbeat. In the centre of the arena stood the frontage of a tall, curved amphitheatre made of stone, with white, fluted columns and many windows and doors placed around its perimeter. High up, between those columns, stood formidable statues cast in bronze. They came to life at random to beckon, wave or point. One blew kisses, another bowed, before transforming into toucans. And once transformed, they called out with rasping, donkey-like cries. Higher still, just below the canvas folds of the marquee roof, a never-ending group of acrobats performed, dressed in green tights and leotards. They worked together in pairs, hanging by their legs from rope swings, before leaping energetically through the air. In mid-flight they would transform into brightly plumed parrots before flying through circular holes in the marquee roof, another pair of acrobats appearing on the rope swing to repeat the process.

Each person walking by in the marquee was dressed in a fancy dress costume: medieval, Victorian, modern, and there was an air of happiness and contentment about all of them. Stave was feeling the same. Wandering between the crowd, strangers would bid him good day or greet him cordially. He espied Dario La, smiling contentedly, pushing a bicycle between the milling people. He was walking past a massive yellow statue that stood as high as the splendid amphitheatre. Surrounding the base of the impressive statue – that of an old man seated, reading a book – stood many lit oil lamps casting their combined ambient glow over the pedestrians strolling by. The statue's face showed benign warmth of spirit and kindness.

Stave went over to it and looked up at its magnificence.

'Amazing, don't you think,' a stranger commented to him. 'A perfect work of art.'

'It certainly is,' Stave replied. 'Who is it?'

'Why, none other than Marcello Sanctifus. He insists we demolish it but then he is a very modest man. We all insist it should stay here in honour of his greatness.'

'I wonder when he will appear at the gathering.'

'We all wonder that too,' the man said and walked away.

Stave did the same and decided to investigate a massive globe of light hovering at the perimeter of the marquee. It sent out bright rays across the passers-by, casting them in daylight.

Then his attention was caught by seeing Quikso Lebum and his seemingly attached lady friend, standing before one of the doors of the amphitheatre. They appeared to be arguing. Mariella was attempting to pull her hand away from Quikso's grip but still without success.

Stave felt he must speak with them again but as he

changed course to do that, a couple barred his way.

'Stave – Stave Swirler? Well I never,' the portly man said, biting his bottom lip, a generous smile growing suddenly. He glanced at the slender woman beside him who gently bowed her head, and she smiled as well, but coyly.

Stave studied them: a small man, with sideburns and a moustache, neatly dressed in what appeared to be Edwardian attire, and his partner – presumably his wife – in a billowing dress that seemed too large for her. She had a way of swaying from side to side as if unsteady on her feet or an affectation of shyness. They looked to each other, still smiling broadly and nodding.

'I'm sorry, but I don't recollect our meeting.'

The man chuckled and with more nodding, he moved forward and patted Stave on the shoulder.

'I'm Berland Understeam and this is my wife, Marigild. Quite simply, we have met you before but you haven't met us yet, until now.'

Stave frowned.

'That doesn't make any sense.'

'Exactly what we said when we met you last time,' replied Berland. 'Time is strange here, isn't it.' His generous smile returned and he nodded again to his wife.

Stave found the constant nodding and smiling to be annoying. He shook his head and rubbed his hair.

'I'm sorry to say but I really don't know what you're talking about,' he replied. At that moment, the globe of light descended upon a group of people to the left of him. Immediately they began to gyrate and twist their limbs, dancing to music only they could hear. 'Anyway, lovely to meet you both but now, if you will excuse me, I need to speak with someone.'

Stave walked quickly away, weaving between the strolling revellers, towards Quikso and Mariella. As he neared them, both standing by one of the large metal and glass double doors set into the amphitheatre, Mariella began pulling Quikso through one of the open doors, a shriek of despair from her.

24 : WHEN DOUBLE IS TROUBLE

STAVE WALKED WITH a fast pace between the crowds of people, as they nodded and smiled to him as though infected by Berland Underwood's affectations, and some said, 'Hello there', 'Good afternoon', or 'A fine morning'. Then he followed Quikso and Mariella through the door of the amphitheatre.

There were fewer people in the large and brightly lit foyer. Two girls fed grass from leather pouches to beautifully painted horses. Those horses were from a fairground ride, free from their roundabout though still with the barley-twist poles sticking from out of their shoulder blades.

After walking across the foyer between the snorting and snuffling animals, he saw Quikso and Mariella at the top of a flight of carpeted stairs.

He was about to follow up when his progress was blocked.

'You can't go up there without a ticket,' a stout man with sideburns said abruptly. He adjusted the lapel on his Edwardian evening suit and looked to his wife who stood beside him as if waiting for affirmation. 'What sort of ticket have you got? Red, pink, blue? Turquoise, I'm guessing.'

'You're Berland Understeam, aren't you?' Stave replied,

ignoring the question. 'Nice to meet you and your wife again after such a short time. But how you got here before me, I'm not sure.'

The man looked confused.

'Have we met before? I don't remember our meeting before. Where have we met before?' he said and he looked to his wife Marigild, as if expecting her to answer.

'In the marquee, a minute ago,' Stave replied.

'That doesn't make sense.'

'That's what you said I said.'

'I'm not certain who you met, sir, but it couldn't have been me. I've been here for hours. Haven't I, dear?'

Marigild merely looked embarrassed and shuffled on the spot in her overlarge dress.

'Perhaps you have a twin? No, I doubt it,' Stave said. 'A time tangle, isn't it. To be expected, the way things are here.'

'A time tangle, indeed, yes, it could be. I've had experience of a few of those in my time, if you excuse the pun,' replied Berland. 'Now then, back to the business of a ticket,' and he put out a hand as if needing it to be shaken.

Stave had learned that part of dream logic was absurdity. With that in mind, he took off his eye mask and placed it in Berland's palm. And without much surprise, the man grinned and said, 'That's fine. Go on through. Don't forget your receipt,' and he handed Stave a round mirror, no more than three inches in diameter.

'Thank you,' Stave said.

He pocketed the mirror, ran up the stairs, and then went through a panelled door into a dimly lit theatre.

Inside were rows of red velvet seats, facing a curtain over

a stage. The curtain looked to be made of a blueish liquid. It undulated and swayed as the lights from the chandeliers – hanging from the wavering patterned ceiling – became brighter before dimming again.

Mariella was standing and wriggling by one of the seats; Quikso pulled her down to sit beside him. Most of the other seats were occupied with chatting spectators, excitedly anticipating the start of a performance. Stave sat on an empty seat behind Quikso and Mariella.

He was about to speak to them when the chandeliers, in their gothic splendour, dimmed further and finally went out. They rotated, before moving across to the cornices of the ornate theatre ceiling.

From each side of the undulating safety curtain, two massive articulated puppets descended – as tall as the theatre stage – made of crudely painted cardboard and timber. They jiggled and wiggled their grotesque faces, their crazy straw hair waving as though in a breeze. Peculiar squawks and squeals emanated from them as if they were conversing in an obscure and unique language. The excited audience patted their knees and as another dream wind blew over Stave, he felt compelled to do the same.

A cardboard cutout of a conductor rose from the orchestra pit.

The curtains dissolved and on the stage, with the sounds of a trumpet, stood a backdrop of a pretty country cottage set in a sunlit woodland. Three simple wooden arches rose up in front of the backdrop.

Stave stood and pointed to the image of the house.

'That is my house, I'm sure of it,' he shouted out.

Feint remembrance of light, of absorption into acceptance of wonderment. But no more. Memories are gone before me – from inner and outer mind again – as quickly as a passing of a fast train.

A man appeared from out of a stage wing, wearing a complete mask made of cardboard. It had a roughly drawn face upon it, painted in grey. He wore blue gloves. He tapped a gloved hand at his anonymous clothing. It evaporated as if it had been some form of ectoplasm, to reveal a turquoise suit.

Why should he be copying my clothing?

With another flourish of hands in blue gloves, his mask was pulled away to reveal another mask, showing the face of Stave Swirler, identical in every detail.

That same face as mine is smiling hideously, with the edges of the mouth touching the corners of the nose. A devil grin, if ever I saw one.

The articulated puppets continued to jiggle and rattle. The imposter spoke evenly, matching Stave's voice tone perfectly.

'Nightmare one. The one nightmare,' the doppelgänger said.

Two angelfish, each five feet or more across, floated onto the stage, nipping at the floorboards. Their eyes looked like whorls of pus. Then guppies the size of terriers came from the theatre wings, growling as they swam in the air in swirls.

This beginning of a nightmare in a dream is becoming wearisome.

The dream wind, previously smelling of lavender, turned into the stench of rotting vegetables. Stave was forgetting even where he was or what he was doing. He felt sick and dizzy but remembered one thing: a copycat was trying to imitate him. He left his theatre seat with an urgency, made his way to the end of the row, walked down the aisle, and up to the stage.

'Why are you copying me? Who are you? What agent are you?' he demanded.

The imposter continued his lunatic grin, and said simply, 'You can never win.'

The watching audience clapped hands on their knees.

'When this dream wind has finished gusting, I will,' Stave replied. 'Let me on stage.'

The audience pounded on their chests like gibbons, some cheering.

I demand to be let on stage so we can sort this out, man to man.

This time, the audience erupted into a tumultuous noise as they stamped their feet on the floor, along with hooting and hollering. The gigantic puppets either side of the stage danced in their grotesque fashion, their unintelligible utterances becoming louder and even more garbled.

There was a poignant pause, an air of expectation, then the whole of the stage descended to ground level with the sounds of pistons firing and the smell of gunshot.

'You'll never remember,' the copycat said.

'Remember what?' Stave shouted as he ran between the footlights onto the stage floorboards. He turned to view the audience who had transformed into mannequins, except for Quikso and Mariella. They were still squabbling in their seats, the yellow glare from the stage lights revolving to light them.

'Remember what?' echoed the duplicate, now at eye level with Stave Swirler. 'That I'm Swave Stirrer?' and he wove in and out of the three arches, before morphing into a limping dog and then scuttled into one of the wings.

'You have to remember for all of us to remember,' Quikso cried out, leaving his seat and pulling Mariella with him along the velvet-carpeted aisle.

'But I only remember so much,' Stave called to him, as his neared. 'Dream winds play tricks with my mind; I keep on forgetting.'

Agents of Tremelon, snapped into Stave's mind. That much he remembered again.

'The agents are becoming stronger. Only they fully remember, and that must change,' Quikso said.

'I'm beginning to understand. This simple dream we are in is becoming a complicated nightmare. But what to do?'

Quikso was near, with Mariella looking solemn at his side.

'We have to stop Tremelon and his evil agents from continuing to overtake,' he said. 'You must not fail to eradicate all of their presences from the realm.'

Now I recall Cassaldra telling me as much.

'But how? Kill them? I can't do that. I've never killed anyone in my life. And I'm not about to start now.'

'No, you must find another way. And anyhow, that's what Tremelon wants you to do.'

'To kill him? But why?'

'Yes, he wants you to kill him,' answered Quikso. 'Because he…'

At that moment, the duplicate Stave Swirler walked out from the stage wing, still wearing a turquoise suit. He went across the bare floorboards of the stage, kicking some of the footlights out of the way and knocking down the cardboard conductor with a casual flick of the arm.

'Enough,' he ordered, his voice no longer matching Stave's, now a grating growl. He pulled off the final mask to expose the sneering features of the former bus driver who had become the maintenance man. He swallowed his double top rows of teeth and another double row appeared straight after. His eyes were still shut. 'Your aura is too bright.' He removed his blue gloves to reveal his crab-like claws. 'You don't wish to follow us, so you are against us. This is your new void, Stave Swirler, and it's about time you were punished – sharp knife, no wife,' he announced.

He looked to the carpet. A lit blowtorch appeared. He picked it up.

So now he can dream summon too...

The chandeliers moved over the ceiling and descended to the seated audience of mannequins, to directly above their motionless heads. The red velvet-covered seats turned to cardboard and they collapsed to the ground, toppling the mannequin audience onto the floor. They crawled away into the corners, leaving a carpeted area with ten large chandeliers at eye level hanging from their thick chains.

A chase started between the chandeliers: the agent of Tremelon ran from one to the other, pushing them into Stave while clutching the blowtorch. His other claw hand snapped open and shut. Stave avoided the swinging chandeliers where possible, keeping his distance from his enemy.

Then the agent stopped. He sneered while he placed the blowtorch onto the stage. He appeared to be concentrating.

He's going to manipulate the dream again...

A long and thick rope, with a noose at each end, fell from the top of the theatre and hung in front of the wooden arches; the nooses had dropped about the ridiculous heads of the large, dancing puppets. The jagged, rattling skeleton of a horse hung upside down from the rope, its hooves tied together with a cord. It gave a pitiful neighing.

'Now you go to nightmare, to the lair,' the former bus driver said and clapped his clawed hands together.

The dream wind became a gusting, evil-smelling gale.

Stave's vision changed in an instant, with a searing pain across his forehead, his heart lurching. He felt his spirit being pulled aggressively from his body.

He tried to resist but it was impossible to fight. He dropped to the ground, feeling the attraction of the horse skeleton as if it were a magnet. He moved towards it on his hands and knees. The puppets leant inwards so that the rope lowered even more, with the horse's spine touching the stage.

'What are you doing?' Quikso said with concern.

'Unable to stop,' Stave answered.

He crawled into the ribcage. A prison of bones.

The puppets stood upright, the skeleton and its captive hanging from the lifted rope above the stage.

Instantly, Stave's spirit moulded to the inside of the skeleton, with utter terror taking him over.

He looked out from the empty eye sockets of the horse skeleton's skull.

My flesh melted into the marrow. Empty of hope; painful limbs; not enough strength to ignore sounds of mocking laughter.

He saw through distressed, clouded vision the ornate

ceiling, and Quikso and Mariella being chased by the agent across the theatre floor. The pair moved with speed between the chandeliers as they attempted to escape. They still held each other's hand.

Mariella cried out the obvious to Stave, as she pulled Quikso to the stage area.

'You have to escape before it's too late!'

But how? As I hover between consciousness and abandonment of mind, I feel the absence of my flesh, my spirit incarcerated within these alien bones. Coldness and darkness descending, aggravating the pervasive aching…yet even more torment is on its way, I know. I feel like I must resign my spirit soon. I have no choice.

Stave spoke in a pained voice but it came out as gurgling as if his vocal cords were made of curdled milk.

'Can't…help…myself.'

Yet he must: with a concerted effort, he made another attempt to be free of his prison. But it was useless.

Quikso had an idea. He ran over to blowtorch, picked it up, then went hurriedly over to the horse skeleton containing the body and spirit of Stave. With his loose hand, he held the blowtorch flame to the cord that bound the hooves to the main rope.

The horse skeleton dropped to the floorboards of the stage with a clatter and Stave was jolted back to his own body. The grotesque puppets lurched forward into the theatre and collapsed into untidy piles.

The agent of Tremelon who had been the bus driver snorted and simply said, 'Next time,' before walking through the middle arch, a black cloth dropping down to cover him.

Stave crawled out of the ribcage.

'What magician trick is that now,' he cried out as he stood. 'Where is he going?'

'Anywhere that you have been before,' Quikso answered. 'Why?'

'To spoil, corrupt, destroy everything which is yours. And if he succeeds, my realm will be next.'

'You talk about realms as if I know what you mean,' said Stave.

'I've been taught each of us have their own realm, all of which have become infiltrated by evil. I've no recollection of my realm but now know I own one.'

'At least we're understanding who the enemy is, although the reason is still a mystery.'

How are you feeling after your ordeal?' Quikso asked.

'Sore inside and unsteady on my feet, thanks for asking. But give me a while, I'll be back to normal. Whatever normal is, where we are.' Stave paused, before adding, 'Tell me, you were going to mention why Tremelon wants me to kill him.'

'Because he knows you can't succeed in that way. He can't die anymore. But by trying to kill him, by giving physical pain to another, you will have failed and lost everything.'

'Then I must learn how to eradicate him from the realms without giving pain?'

'Precisely,' Quikso said. 'Are you feeling ill? You don't look well; you're shivering.'

Stave still shuddered from the horrifying experience in the horse skeleton.

'I'm OK, thanks, settling down. What to do now to solve these terrible situations?'

Mariella interrupted.

'How to solve my terrible situation first.'

'And what would that be?' Stave asked.

She brought her hand and arm from behind her back and Stave understood immediately why they were seen to be constantly holding hands. Their fingers and palms were fused together.

'You see now?' she said.

'How did that happen?'

'Another of Tremelon Zandar's nightmares. He's getting imaginative,' Quikso said. 'We've tried everything we can think of but it seems we're stuck together for good.'

Stave thought for a moment.

'What's needed is dream logic,' he answered. 'I understand the principles now. To believe something will happen is sometimes enough.'

Quikso sighed with impatience.

'Sorry, but don't you think we want to be free of this? No matter how hard we believe it, we can't separate. And don't tell me we're not believing enough.'

'Then we must try something else. Here's my dream logic: hug each other.'

'What do you mean?'

'Simply that – hug each other,' Stave repeated. 'Make sure the rosettes are close, with the fused hands in between.'

'It can't be as easy as that but it's worth a try. Mariella, do you mind?'

'I'm quite fed up with you already – as long as you don't overdo it.'

With a slightly embarrassed and awkward hug, they

ensured the fused hands were between the rosettes. And after, their hands were separated.

Mariella said with a relieved smile, 'Thank you so much.'

'You're welcome,' Stave replied.

'Yes, thanks, far easier than I'd thought possible,' Quikso said.

There was a pause before Stave asked, 'What do we know about Tremelon Zandar?'

'Not much, only that he is a different person for everyone; that he loves snakes—'

'What sort of snakes?' Mariella asked.

'Any sort,' Quikso continued. 'It's a similar feature within most of his nightmare scenarios. And he likes to torture people, with snakes in particular. For certain, our reality will become even more of a bad dream if we allow him and the agents to continue. We have to make it our good dream in reality, to stabilise our world which has been stolen from us. We must decide our next course of action.'

'I've decided,' Stave answered. 'I'm going to follow the agent. I suggest you two stay here.'

Mariella raised her eyebrows but nodded all the same.

'I'll come with you,' Quikso said.

'I'd prefer to go it alone, if you don't mind,' Stave replied. 'Providing the gathering is clear, I suggest you join those others who are waiting for the arrival of Marcello Sanctifus. Or if not, stay in the marquee again. You'll be safe there. I will follow the agent to find Tremelon Zandar.'

Further into the dream territory gone bad.

He went over to the middle wooden arch and pushed aside the dust-covered curtain.

25 : ALONG AND DOWN

A LONG CORRIDOR was exposed beyond, consisting of grey walls and floor, dimly lit, with patches of ice upon them.

Stave stepped forward and turned back to the curtain hanging from the arch. But it had gone – in its place stood another grey wall. Attached to that was a brass hook.

Immediately, he sensed a depressing atmosphere descend.

My mind is grey because of these walls. Or is it the other way around? Oppressive, despite the coldness. But I must continue, to find Tremelon Zandar. He is despicable for what he's doing to me and others. It must stop. Don't know how yet, but I will find a way, I swear.

He began walking along the chilly corridor, checking the walls for any exits. The corridor seemed monotonous, lacking variation, and endless. A place devoid of imagination or creativity. Above was a sombre sky smeared with purple streaks.

He looked ahead. Another frosty corridor led off to the right. He went swiftly to it, rubbing his cold hands together. Upon turning the corner, he saw a simple table at the end. It stood against a back wall with an unidentified object upon its polished top.

While striding towards the table, he avoided areas of frost and ice on the grey floor. More corridors branched off from the one he walked along. He guessed there might be a labyrinth of corridors.

Strange whisperings came from above, similar to those which had emanated from the door mouths encountered within the keepers of the chasm's domain. He looked up and saw the mannequins – those that had been the theatre audience – gazing down to him with unblinking stares.

Stave reached the end of the corridor.

On the table stood a cardboard model of the stage he had left behind, the size of a shoe box, stylised in every detail. The cardboard arches stood no more than two inches high. The stage lights were a row of beads, the marionettes at the sides, just cutouts made from thick paper. Even the horse skeleton hanging by its hooves from the rope was there, small and made from cardboard, painted in silver. Laying below it stood a tiny cardboard box and a trapdoor.

In this version, the stage backdrop of the cottage in the woods was a framed painting. Stave picked it up to study it more closely. He turned it over: there was ring on the back.

He knew he must hang the painting on the first wall with the brass hook on it, although not quite certain why. However, in this dream environment, it seemed a sensible course of action.

Dream logic again.

With the picture firmly in his grasp, he walked slowly back along the grey and cold corridor, inspecting the lifeless walls as he did so, sometimes peering into the other corridors leading off. They all seemed as featureless as each other.

More whispering from the mannequins. Then, joining that sound were clattering, clacking and squawking noises.

He turned the corner into the first corridor to see the skeleton horse trotting towards him in an ungainly fashion. Blue steam came from the skull's nostril holes. Its eye sockets were filled with maggots and in its ribcage squirmed snakes of different lengths and markings.

It broke into a canter and began to shriek, heading towards Stave, who stepped back into the side corridor with a nimble step. The bony entity galloped past.

Stave turned quickly left into the main corridor, looking back to see the nightmare creation disappearing into the distance.

A sudden thought came to Stave's mind, that the corridors were his coffin, a wicked maze with no exits, and that he was trapped without food or water. Not that he had thought about eating or drinking since entering the tunnel on the bus those hours ago.

Upon reaching the beginning of the first corridor, he hung the small painting onto the hook on its back wall. And as he did so, the wall moved back slightly. He continued to push the wall, a sense of the unreal enveloping him. He was extending the grey painted corridor, the more he pushed. It was easy to move, only the minimum pressure required by pressing his palms to it.

He exposed long cardboard boxes, the height and width of coffins, standing at regular intervals, inset into the side walls. In each one stood a cardboard articulated figure. Their hands and feet were together as if laid to rest standing upright. Their cardboard faces showed eyes shut, scrawled in black, and mouths turned downward, painted roughly with grey paint.

After he had pushed the end wall another fifteen feet, he exposed a thin lift with its single door open, standing on the right-hand wall.

He inspected it with suspicion. But still, it seemed the only means of escape…

He stepped inside and turned to face the corridor with its lines of boxes. The figures inside them twitched and jerked. He was about to press one of the buttons in the lift but before he could, the door slid over of its own accord and plunged him into semi-darkness. Only the bulbs from a control panel gave out light as they glowed in neon, showing the numbers seven to one. He pressed one of them but there was no movement, only the sound of sarcastic chuckling. None of the other numbers worked either, except to promote the same mirth.

Stifling. Trapped, going from bad to worse.

Stave became claustrophobic, and worriedly shouted, 'Got to get out,' and he beat upon the sides of the lift.

Only then did he notice an unlit button, further down the side, marked with the letter "H".

He pressed it with urgency despite a gnawing feeling that his situation could only worsen.

I could be sending myself to Tremelon Zandar's hell. Why is heaven always above and hell below? Then what manner is hell when different for everyone? Is it banal to say that my life might flash before me? Then at least I'll remember my life…

Immediately, the lift shuddered with an excruciating sound as if nails were being scratched across a blackboard.

Then the sensation of moving down in the cold metal box.

After a few minutes, Stave convinced himself he would be travelling downwards forever. But just as he thought this, the lift came to a sudden halt and the door slid open. Orange light bathed him. Stave stepped into the interior of a vandalised cottage.

26 : WITNESSING A DAY TERROR

FROM WITHIN THE interior of the rubbish-strewn living room, Stave peered out of one of the smashed leaded windows to the outside. Deep orange light from the sun that was like a gold plate scratched with lacerations streamed through the damaged panes of the derelict cottage. Grey birds hung in the air over a wide expanse of blackened earth, within a valley barren of life. Parched grass turned yellow on the hills somehow avoided the sun's orange rays. And all around the rim of the valley crept dark blue filaments under the contaminated sky. The soil was furrowed at random with craters and piles of earth desecrating it. Between those craters and piles, tree stumps lay, their trunks strewn between them. In the distance an object reflected the light, glowing as if a candle flame.

Looking back to the inside, Stave viewed with dismay the damage to the living room. Part of the ceiling including some of the oak beams had fallen in one corner in rough mounds. Battens from the walls lay on the rolled-up carpet along with peeled wallpaper and the dusty mess. The rugs had been stuffed into holes in the exposed floorboards. Stave identified the upturned settee and mahogany sideboard, pulled to the floor and strewn with debris. They belonged to him.

Sudden recognition now. This is my cottage, my dwelling. But with so much ruination; I feel despair…

And upon going into the sitting room, he found more destruction – chairs were upturned, shelves ripped from the walls, desk broken and drawers scattered on the floor. His modest library was no better, with books ripped from the bookcases and laying on the defiled carpet in untidy heaps, some with pages ripped from them, others half-burned.

Perhaps the damage to his property was an attempt to damage his psyche? If that was the case, it had succeeded as a dark mood overtook him, as if even his mind was being covered by fallen beams and dust.

The pine kitchen door had been pulled from its hinges and lay flat on the floor.

Stave heard grating voices, and clicking and grunting.

He reticently peered into the kitchen, hiding behind the wall and one of the doorposts. Two agents of Tremelon wearing full masks sat opposite each other at the kitchen table. One of the masks showed the closed eyes of a woman in her thirties, while the other, a man of similar age. They sat with grey bibs around their necks, knives and forks held upright on the table each side of their grey, square plates.

Above them, the beams in the kitchen ceiling were groaning and breathing as if an alive creature.

Stave stepped back into the sitting room with its destroyed library. He must leave immediately. But then he heard seemingly normal voices and was intrigued. Furtively, he looked around the doorframe again to the kitchen interior.

The woman at the sink draining board stood preparing

salad vegetables; the man, by the wall cupboards next to the fridge, stuffed a chicken with chunks of red meat on the works surface. Both had their backs to Stave.

'How are we doing, my dearest Tacie? Getting there?' the standing man said.

'Oh yes, I particularly love this dream,' the woman by the sink replied while slicing a stick of celery into small pieces. 'Although I really don't understand why you are wearing cardboard shoes.'

The man turned to her with a pleasant smile. Stave recognised him: it was Konie. He realised that the mask worn by one the agents matched Konie's face precisely.

'The same reason your right hand is turning to cardboard,' Konie said, his smile growing the more but eyes showing grief.

'Oh, that's making sense,' Tacie replied and she laughed, and continued laughing. She turned around. Her face was a laughing version of the other agent of Tremelon's placid mask.

'You can stop laughing now,' Konie said. 'I have finished stuffing the chicken horse.'

At those words, Stave felt something taken from the pit of his stomach. Then something given: a dull aching and sickness starting. The situation seemed deeply disturbing.

Tacie immediately stopped laughing and took hold of a tomato in her left hand. She closed her eyes, this time with no laughter, her facial features relaxed, mouth slightly downturned, matching precisely one of the agent's masks.

A grey shadow fell over the windowsill and a whispering came from outside, dull, like the shadow.

That you, dear?' Tacie asked.

'The beautiful voice? Or the uncanny whispers? Or the beautiful life, as is? 'Tis not my doing, fair one. How's the salad now? Managing with your arm turning to cardboard? Rather worrying.'

'What is, dearest?'

'The cat, stepping quickly on the railings, without a head or tail,' Konie said with distress.

'But that's all down to me, I'm almost certain. My dream takes funny turns sometimes. I feel the presence of a never-ending void from without and within.'

'How poetic of you, dear Tacie. From without and within. I know not which. Isn't it the most real dream you've ever had? Like reality, only more real, don't you think?'

'I agree. I even feel cold all over now. Colder than I've ever felt before. Though I'm embracing it like I should – the colder I feel, the warmer I feel. The warmer I feel, the colder I get. Our eminent visitors are encouraging it. My entrails are…'

'Don't be mucky, dearest one,' replied Konie. 'Stick to the salad. Eventually, you will be sensationless in the body and mind, like they told us. Can't hurt, only temporary, they said. Effects of dreamtime, that's what they told me; then the restored cottage given to us as they promised.'

'You are funny. Even my cardboard arm and hand are funny.'

'They are. You've grey paint spilled on them, in spatters.'

'So I do,' said Tacie. Her face changed to wide-mouthed fear as if she were witnessing a dreadful horror and she whined, 'Help me, dear.'

The agent with Tacie's face showing on his mask began to take the mask off but upon Konie answering, the agent's crab claw hands picked up the cutlery again.

'Slice the tomato for you?'

'Of course, loved one,' she said with a sob in her voice. 'But mind the snakes on the floor.'

'What snakes would they be, Tacie? I can't see any snakes.'

Konie left his place by the refrigerator and hobbled over to his wife.

'Foot's playing up,' he muttered. When next to Tacie, he picked up a knife and began to slice the tomato. 'Keep going, keep going,' he said, with anxiety in his voice. When he had pressed the knife down to the middle of the fruit, he stopped, and announced, 'Something inside.' He peeled off the cut slice from the half of tomato which had turned grey, and retrieved two tiny bronze feathers from its pipped centre. 'Out the window, there they go, where this dream's going, nobody knows,' he said as he opened the window above the sink and threw the objects out. 'There, all done for you, dear. You've still got to chop, chop, chop more celery,' he added.

Tacie looked past him to where he had been standing, and said in return, 'But first, you still have to finish stuffing the chicken horse,' and she began laughing again. 'Is that what they called it? Am I right? Was I right at some time? When can we dislike this dream, dear?'

Stave became increasingly disturbed. He sensed that behind her happy face was another with a look of horror, covered as if her real face was a mask after all, like the agents sitting like mannequins at the kitchen table.

Then the dull, staccato voice of one of the agents, 'Don't.

Hurry. Don't. Be. Quicker.'

He was uncertain whether or not to confront the evil pair. Then he decided that if he did, it could put Konie's and Tacie's lives at risk.

Not knowing of any way to help them from inside the cottage, he backed into the destroyed library. From there, he returned to the living room, opened the front door, and went outside into the unusual sunlight. Perhaps he could convince the couple to escape via the back door after talking quietly to them from outside the kitchen window.

27 : LANDSCAPE OF MIRAGE ECHOES

FROM THE FRONT steps of the cottage, Stave peered at the barren landscape devoid of features, bathed in the hot, orange light.

He tried to recall what had been there before. A forest, that much he did remember, but now all that remained of it were the scarred tree trunks laying on their sides with shrivelled leaves, and stumps scattered across the dark earth.

After going around to the side of the building – the epicentre of the barren landscape – he came to a simple gate, and opened it. From there, he made his way around to the kitchen window. While bending to avoid being seen by the agents of Tremelon, he picked up the bronze feathers and placed them into his trousers pocket with the others.

He bobbed his head up in the hope of talking to Konie and Tacie through the window but he was too late. Both of them had turned into grey-painted cardboard. He was overcome with a deep sadness.

He went back around the cottage, through the wooden gate and returned to the dead earth of the front garden. And after looking out across the melancholic landscape, he began walking towards the distant hills, weaving his way between the tree stumps.

He accidentally kicked one of them – it gave a bell-like sound, emitting its remarkable golden tone for a minute.

Purity, like a delicate hum of the divine.

On he trudged, avoiding the random piles of soil, and craters indenting the earth. There was a pungent smell of smoke and ash in the cloying air.

Occasionally, he came across sealed cardboard boxes with grey ticks marking their sides. He was tempted to open them but resisted when, upon touching any one of them, it clicked like a Geiger counter.

As he trod across the demolished woodland, he became increasingly concerned at not remembering anything other than from the moment he entered the tunnel a while ago. Three hours before, six or ten even? The announcer at the gathering was right, time seemed malleable, flexible in these dreamscapes.

Around him were mirages. A stone and wood pavilion, piles of moss-covered boulders, antiquated rose bowls carved from marble, a waterfall, a beautifully landscaped garden – all seen as out-of-focus light reflections.

As soon as he walked through a mirage object, it would fade as easily as a phantom.

He sat on one of the tree stumps.

To be without memory was frustrating. If only he could recall what the mirages meant to him.

The words "Love and Beauty" came to mind. If ever there were such fine qualities, he considered they had long gone from this place.

A vibrancy missing, frequencies lost, now that the beauty is destroyed.

Only repellant thoughts of means of destruction remaining. Innocent people's soul taken, leaving wrecked bodies before spirit desecration.

He stood and trekked on over the damaged soil, avoiding the holes, those large enough to have been caused by explosions or the impact of small meteors.

The orange sun was debilitating – the further on he walked, the more its rays dried his mouth and sapped energy from his already tired limbs.

The legacy of the blistering tangerine.

He considered he was thirsty and thought as much. Immediately, a wooden bowl filled with water stood within one of the smaller craters.

Dream summoning. It worked well again this time. Cassaldra would be pleased with me.

Stave accepted the existence of thought made real easily. A vague memory sprang to mind of mental energies brought into physicality being a normal part of his existence.

The mysterious sea of the unconscious mind.

He slid down to the bottom of the crater but as soon as his hand reached out, the bowl was dragged into the earth by a swarm of metallic snakes, the size of worms. Each one emitted blue smoke from its tiny, fanged jaws. One of the creatures landed on his thumb and straightaway the skin there began to blister. He shook it off and clambered out of the crater.

He visualised the bowl of water again, wishing for it with all of his mental energy, and it appeared at the periphery of his vision. But as soon as he went over to the bowl to take hold of it, that too was dragged into the black soil by the writhing, worm-like snakes.

A vibrating explosion occurred from behind that seemed to tremble the very earth. Stave turned back to see the cottage wreathed in blue flames.

Alarm gripped his throat, already dried from the orange sun. He licked his dried lips with a parched tongue and stumbled onward. His cottage had been totally destroyed. He looked back again, now seeing only a massive brown cardboard box where the cottage had been, a large grey tick marking its side.

More snakes – this time, the size of pythons and made of blue smoke – slithered fast across the dismal field, away from the destroyed cottage. They weaved around the stumps of the trees, down and up the craters, and over the piles of crumbled earth.

They're moving too fast for me to escape...

A casement window appeared above him, hovering in the orange-lit sky.

Dream logic is required again.

A ladder, he thought. He retrieved the tiny ladder and the magnifying glass from his jacket pocket.

He magnified the ladder with the glass, the same way he had done with the objects underwater in the underground station. He di the same several times until the full-size ladder lay on the ground. He ran to it and picked it up. Once he had stood it vertically, he leant the top of it on the sill of the widow. While climbing up, he looked over the barren landscape to the smoke creatures coming ever closer. Should any one of them touch him, he knew that would be the beginning of the end, an experience worse even than his spirit trapped in the bones of a horse.

When he reached the top of the ladder, the window opened to show a beautiful courtyard lit by a full moon, with a night sky above.

28 : CHARMED BY DELIGHTFULNESS

HE PEERED THROUGH the window. There were high walls to be seen. They were decorated with flower baskets overflowing with beautiful flowers within containers in the shapes of birds, and lion heads containing magnificent shrubs.

In the middle of the courtyard stood a fountain, the centrepiece of it a shoal of fish, slowly spinning. Surrounding it were white stone columns and upon each one stood a statue in a metal cage. One of the placid statues moved slowly as if shedding the constraints of cold stone.

'I sensed you were in danger. I have managed to intersect again,' the young woman said from her cage. 'I must be quick, though. Here in one of our special places, Tremelon Zandar is near. I can feel the cowbell vibrating.'

One of our places?

Stave looked to her with a quizzical expression.

Do you know Cassaldra?' he asked.

'I am Cassaldra.'

'How can you be? She is a much older lady.'

He gazed at her attractive face. For a fraction of a second, with heart lurching, there was recognition, then it was gone.

'Have you believed all I've told you so far?' she said.

As good an explanation as any.

'Yes, I have.'

'Then you must believe me when I tell you this: you are my husband, also known as Marcello Sanctifus, amongst other names.'

Stave shook his head.

'That is preposterous. You told me Marcello Sanctifus is an old man. I am under thirty. At least I think I am.'

'It is too much for you to consider at once,' Cassaldra continued. 'I'm sorry I had to tell you now; I should have waited. Another part of the nightmare created by Tremelon Zandar – I am seen as an old woman when I'm a young woman; and vice versa.'

'So I'm also an old man and also a young man? And you are a young and old woman – at the same time?'

'Leave time for another day for when we meet again. Hopefully in our cottage, when the nightmare is over.'

'So I live with you in the cottage?' Stave said.

'A humble cottage is one of the places we choose to live unless that has been captured by Tremelon Zandar as well.'

'Yes, captured and destroyed,' Stave answered with sadness.

'It can all be back as it was again, you have to believe me. You will learn how to repair once he has been defeated. For the while, I must soon keep quiet. One thing is for certain, to defeat him will be easy.'

'Why do you say that?'

'Because he and his agents are bound by the dreams despite them turning to nightmares. Dream logic, like scientific logic, is unassailable; it cannot be undone or conquered. You will find a way to set yourself free again.'

'But what about you? How can I help to free you?'

'You have no choice but to continue deeper into your own mind which has become Tremelon Zandar's mind,' Cassaldra explained. 'Once he has been defeated, I will be free, as you will be. The dreamscapes within your realm and beyond have been damaged enough.'

Beyond the realm. Other realms, as Quikso mentioned; other dreamscapes. Other realms without dreamers?

'You will learn more soon enough.' Now the cowbells sounded about Cassaldra's and Stave's necks, with their dry clunks. 'Tremelon is listening, so I must go. I bid you farewell, my love.'

'My love?' replied Stave.

Cassaldra's sight misted with tears.

'Yes, Stave. I love you with all my heart and have done so for a long time. Goodbye, and I hope to see you again soon.'

The courtyard became obscured when fierce flames covered the window – hot despite being made of paper – and Stave was alone again.

A yearning for Cassaldra jolted throughout his being. Yet how could a stranger be so familiar a spirit?

Most of the smoke serpents across the field had disintegrated into clouds of grey and blue, and drifted into the orange sky. The few remaining slithered around the bottom of the ladder, and whichever part of the ladder they touched, it turned to cardboard and began to collapse with his weight.

Ahead was the object catching the fierce orange light, now glowing as if on fire.

29 : MOCKING OF MARCELLO SANCTIFUS

As STAVE BEGAN climbing down, he cried out, 'Yes, see you again soon, I must,' and as the window above him vanished, he felt a sense of loss.

He reached the bottom of the ladder just as it collapsed and as the last of the smoke snakes evaporated.

There was an explosive round of applause. Two lines of people wearing eye masks stood not far ahead of him on the churned ground. Stave recognised some of them as the ones captured at the gathering. They huddled together with expectant faces as if waiting for something to happen or someone to appear. Stave kept his distance from them.

Then, without warning, a blue disc in the sky began to overlap the orange sun – no less than an eclipse, happening at a fast rate. A direful searing noise rent the air as if the sun was being erased permanently. The masked people clapped more, with some cheering and whistling.

Stave wanted to move on but being intrigued by their behaviour, he waited.

The orange sunlight lessened by the second until finally the process was complete. All were bathed in deep blue.

With the barren landscape plunged into cold light, some

of the guests lit lanterns mounted on poles and all stood silently, in anticipation of the next event to occur.

The horse skeleton, with snakes still writhing in its ribcage, appeared from out of the dark blue into the light of the lanterns. Thick lengths of rope from its shoulder blades were attached to the front bumper of a wheelless car. The skeleton dragged the dilapidated vehicle behind it across the darkened soil.

A sound of a drum struck at regular intervals, the lantern light dimming and brightening in time with the beat. And those without lanterns clapped slowly and starting a chant of "Sanctifus, Sanctifus, Sanctifus—"

Another nightmare unfolding.

A shuddering of air, like the last gasps of a dying man. The light from the lamps flickered across the hopeful faces as the skeleton horse ceased pulling, and the rusting heap of metal came to a halt.

With difficulty, an old man climbed out of one of the car's passenger seats. His wrinkles resembled the bark of a tree, his eyes burning with fierce passion yet filled with grief. His silver hair was covered by a large, dark blue teapot, worn upside down as a hat. He pulled it from his head and flung it away but another appeared immediately after.

The old man's features were familiar to Stave: his heart gave a jolt when he realised that perhaps he was looking at an ancient version of himself.

On the old man's back, weighing him down so he stooped, was a massive crab, its pincers around his frail neck. Every time he appeared to want to speak, the pincers tightened about him, dull grey sparks emanating from it.

'Sanctifus, Sanctifus, Sanctifus,' the crowd continued, the chant now low and forbidding.

The humiliation of this man is terrible. Already I feel the weight of the massive crab on my back, its pincers tightening about my neck, and firm pressure on my head from an invisible pot. There's nothing I can do to help – I must escape before the nightmare worsens...

Stave stepped quickly away from the crowd, the old man, decrepit car and horse skeleton. He glanced back to see the dream of Sanctifus attempting to retrieve body organs that were dropping from his chest and stomach. With a sharp pain in his own chest, Stave fled from them all.

Over the earth he went, with day turned to night. And looking back he saw the spectacle behind him, now like a bonfire of blue flames.

As he stumbled further on across the dark field, the blue disc began to fade, until the glaring orange sunlight returned with all its fiery strength.

Once more, the unknown object ahead of him glinted.

30 : FLIGHT TO WORSE

THE CLOSER HE got to the object, the more detail he could make out. And when no more than ten feet away, he could see a shining semicircle of polished metal, the size of a van. There were studs around its perimeter and a line of holes at one end, poking above a mound of earth. Stave went further towards it and around the mound.

He found an identical semicircle of metal there, and realised they were wings, both attached to the sides of a substantial barrel of brass that was studded with copper rivets. A silver pipe came from one end of the barrel. Attached to that, a copper sphere was mounted, representing a head. And on the head were metal rings forming brass eyes, and an iron beak. All together the construction was a large, metal bird. It looked an impressive contraption as it still glowed in the glare of the orange sun.

Inset in the side of its body – the brass barrel – was a hinged door. Stave opened it and climbed inside, and sat on a polished metal seat. The door closed of its own accord and a green light lit the interior. The only controls were two buttons marked "on" and "off". There were two lenses set ahead, together like a pair of binoculars. Stave looked through them and saw outside to the destroyed landscape.

After inspecting the interior more, he found a copper jug under the seat, filled with fresh water. He took it and drank greedily.

Feeling refreshed, he was even more refreshed by an unusual coolness within the cabin, lessening the temperature of his hot brow.

He pressed the button marked "on".

Immediately there was juddering, the whole contraption moving up and down with the squeaking and quaking of metal. Through small glass panels on both sides, he could see the stubs moving as though the metal bird attempted to fly.

Stave opened the door and got out. A strange machine, he considered, and one which had failed if the intention was to launch into the sky.

He was about to walk away to investigate the other side of the valley when a particular thought occurred to him. Dream rules could be applied again.

A solution to the flying device unable to take off was conceived: he took out the sixteen tiny wings from his trousers pocket. Then, after retrieving the magnifying glass from his waistcoat, he placed the wings on the ground, spaced widely apart. Once that was accomplished, he inspected each feather with the magnifying glass, pulling back to see the object larger and larger until he had every one of them the size of an adult arm. The process hadn't taken long. They were all beautifully detailed, each with a nib of metal at one end of them.

He lifted them up, one at a time. They were surprisingly

heavy. He went over to the metal bird and attached eight of the feathers by placing the nibs into the holes on one of the wings then repeated the process on the other one.

He opened the door of the metal bird and climbed into it once more, leaving the orange sunlight behind. As he sat, the green light glowed and after he had pressed the "on" button, the bird pumped its wings with singing of metal. But instead of flying into the parched sky, the contraption began burrowing into the earth, using the articulated feathers much as a mole might.

Down the metal bird went, its great metal wings churning the soil as they flapped, with spurts of boiling water spitting from its beak and oil seeping from its eyes. On it went through layers of the earth, past ancient and unknown artefacts, and cavernous areas with underground rivers, until it reached a clear space, and dropped to a stratum of rock.

31 : SEWER OF BAD DREAMS

HE WAS EXHILARATED after the ride into the earth and sat for a minute within the cabin of the metal bird.

Finally, he opened the small door and got out, jumping down from the rock that the contraption had landed upon.

He found himself in a red-brick sewer, with the sounds of dripping water coming from arches of granite. There was a distinct stench of rotting fruit. Down the centre of the sewer ran oily, blue liquid in a wide gulley. A paper aeroplane floated on it. Burning torches lit the morbid place.

Stave walked slowly onwards. The noise of his footsteps echoed.

He felt despondent all of a sudden, still trapped in another bad dream. How had he felt fine within the metal bird yet here, within a larger space, claustrophobia pressed in on him? He longed for a return to normality.

He discovered a tunnel leading off to his left from the main sewer. He heard shuffling and the beating of wings. Intrigued, he entered the tunnel and went between the damp, roughly hewn stone walls. Grey-blue limpets moved slowly over their uneven surfaces, exposing or covering pairs of eyes. Some of those eyes were tearful, aggressive or apathetic, others sorrowful or depressed. They blinked at random, following Stave's movements as he walked through puddles of water.

The essence of memory only – gentleness and peaceful existence, even in my dream life; day to day happenings filled with joy and calmness. This I must hold in my mind as hope.

There must be no resigned acceptance of his situation. He heaved a sigh of determination. He would manipulate the dream, whether it be his or someone else's.

Before he could consider what to do next, he found a seagull at the end of the tunnel, its orange beak cruelly bound with wire.

'Come here, bird, let me take that off for you,' Stave said and bent down to it. But it flapped its wings and skipped out of the way. 'It's for your own good.'

Stave ran after the bird and cornered it. He lunged for it before it took flight and managed to grab hold of its body. Holding it tightly under one arm, he untwisted the wire and placed the bird back onto the ground.

It opened wide its orange beak but instead of the usual screeching seagull call, it began to howl like a demented demon, blue smoke emitting from it that curled in the air towards him.

Stave ran from it and out of the side tunnel into the main brick-lined sewer again.

He ran into a soft mass – a portly man, dressed as a butler.

'Don't mind me,' the man said, holding onto the glass of liquid that had rocked on the silver tray. 'I was only trying to help.'

'How were you trying to help?' Stave asked.

'In your adventure. But that seems long gone. As a proud member of the dream cast…'

'You're very solid for dream cast.'

The shadows shivered from the light of the flickering torches along the brick walls.

'Would we want it any other way? As I was saying, as a proud member of dream cast I would like to congratulate you for getting this far into the dream adventure. Have a glass of whatever you enjoy drinking.'

The butler offered the tray with the drink upon it to Stave.

'No thanks, and anyway, It looks like water. And I'm not thirsty anymore, I've just had some.'

'Ah, but it will taste of your favourite tipple, sir.'

'No, really, although I'm sure it would. You spoke of a dream adventure – this is far from an adventure. I'm trapped in a bad dream heading towards a nightmare. All of Tremelon Zandar's doing, you must know.'

'Is that so?' the butler said. 'No wonder I haven't seen an adventurer in a while, and the private party in the mansion house vanished.'

'Sounds mighty grand, in the mansion house, I mean.'

'Oh it certainly is, sir, with guests of the wonderful and magnanimous Marcello Sanctifus. Everyone partaking in a wondrous dream adventure. The house has beautiful objects to be seen, magnificent gardens too, including the maze of delights. I am a good butler there, one of the best. I was given the honour of butler of the year award, two years ago. Can I direct you to the orangery?'

'If you're talking about the orangery I've seen, it's dilapidated, derelict in the extreme,' Stave replied. 'As for the mansion house…' He stopped from speaking further.

'That is a shame. Yes, such a shame.'

'More destruction by the agents of Tremelon.'

'Then you don't want a drink and no need to be directed anywhere?'

'Unless you know where this sewer tunnel leads?'

'Let me see now – I do remember, and bear with me, this is from the back of my mind – to avoid a bad dream you have to avoid any sewers, amongst other places. But then that's a bit late now, isn't it?'

'Just a bit,' Stave replied. 'Right, I'll carry on, see if I can avoid any more badness along the way, although I doubt it. Nice to meet you.'

But there was no reply from the butler: he had turned into a wooden carving.

As Stave carried on along the sewer tunnel, he pondered on the adventure game that was no more. He guessed that if he was Marcello Sanctifus, then he had been instrumental in organising the adventure. But with his loss of memory, there was no way of knowing for sure.

The torches along the walls distracted his train of thought. Their flames doubled in size with bursts and a whooshing, and lit the tunnel no less brightly than the orange sun had shone light over the barren landscape above.

A mass of butterflies of all shapes and sizes appeared from the walls and they squeaked like bats. They fluttered and twirled until their colourful wings began dropping from them, the bodies of the insects now no more than wriggling black slugs, falling into the blue stream.

Ahead of him were dark blue rats with extended legs, their

bodies bigger than cats. They appeared ungainly as if on stilts and they scampered along like four-legged spiders. They seemed more afraid of Stave than he was of them; they disappeared into the shadows. They took the light with them. The brightly burning torches extinguished all at once and Stave was plunged into darkness. He felt his way along one of the brick walls.

Two glowing figures advanced upon him. He froze where he was, his skin crawling from the startling sight of them. Then he attempted to get away by patting the wall and inching backwards in the blackness. Those mannequins without faces, lit as if from neon, were quickly upon him. They dragged him from the safety of the wall and along the tunnel. He could hear them breathing deeply with harsh, rasping inhalations and exhalations. Their grip either side of him was strong. As much as he struggled, he couldn't be free of them.

Further along, an area of the sewer glowed blue. The mannequins forced Stave into a wheelbarrow. After taking a handle of the barrow each, they pushed him forward into that blue glare.

An agent of Tremelon stood over an open sarcophagus. On the sides of the sarcophagus were images of crabs, carved in relief. Along one wall stood blue lanterns on poles, casting the blue light. And along the opposite wall were rows of standing, open caskets, with a grey mannequin in each, their hands clasped together.

'Ashes. To. Dust. Dust. To. Dirt. Dirt. To. Muck. Muck. To. Filth,' the agent said, adjusting his mask, a series of visages appearing upon it, one after the other. He indicated with one of his crab claw hands and the mannequins tipped Stave unceremoniously from the wheelbarrow onto the floor's blue bricks.

'Don't. Stand. Up,' the agent said in his guttural and staccato voice.

Rather than be on the floor, Stave did as he was asked, brushing himself down, although his turquoise suit and leather shoes were still immaculate.

Straight away the two mannequins – who had pushed the wheelbarrow – manhandled him over to the sarcophagus. One pushed him in the back, the other lifted one of his legs, both attempting to tip him into it. As the sarcophagus filled with squirming snakes, the bottom of it gave way and the serpents fell downwards into a dark void.

'Yes, I know what you want me to do,' Stave cried out, 'but I'm not going to do it.'

Trepidation had overtaken him but he knew he must get away. He wheeled around and ran as fast as he was able from the stone sarcophagus and its nightmarish creatures, into the semi-darkness ahead.

Further on there was a ladder set in the side of the sewer wall. He heard the mannequins clattering after him. Stave went to it and climbed up as quickly as he could. Set in the ceiling was a trapdoor. He was certain it would lead him to another chapter of a nightmare journey. But he had no choice. He pushed on the trapdoor and it opened easily.

32 : EMPTY STREETS OF DESOLATION

STAVE CLIMBED UP and out of the trapdoor onto floorboards of an empty room. The floorboards were made of cardboard. There was no door. However, there was a window without a pane of glass, set in one of the mildew-covered cardboard walls. With suspicion, he looked out of the paneless window to an empty street of a desolate town. Brown tenement buildings were there in rows, some standing three or four stories high. Rooftops in the distance showed light brown chimney stacks, higher buildings poked above the dismal tenements. The steeple of a church and the tops of a museum and other corporate buildings could be seen; all of them made from murky, brown cardboard.

Chiming of a clock, its bells sounding as if a recording played backwards.

He climbed through the window, dropping down onto a cardboard pavement.

The cardboard road was pitted with holes and jagged gashes, and covered with puddles of a blue, tar-like liquid. Human hearts made of stone were scattered upon it, chipped or broken. Now the sound of barking from afar, like coughing but reversed, wild and animal-like. The sky was grey with an endless repetition of stormy clouds slowly drifting like billows of fog. All was sucked of life. An air of deadness and coldness and despair, every building and street seemingly deserted and abandoned. A tenseness hung in the atmosphere like an unseeable mantle, with a formidable grip over the barren environment.

Despair all around. A cloying atmosphere, seeming to clot my blood even, so sluggish do I feel. Fright overtaking too, though I'm not certain why I should be frightened of empty cardboard tenements.

Stave walked with suspicion along one of the brown and lifeless pavements, noticing details like cardboard doors, with cardboard door knockers and letterboxes, and cardboard window frames. Some of those were boarded over with more cardboard, others without glass or covering of any kind. Plain brown cardboard lamps lined the pavement. A cardboard bike lay abandoned in the rutted road.

Why does this town seem familiar? Perhaps I do know it well; maybe it's another memory deleted from my mind.

The imposing street was long. The cardboard buildings either side seemed to lean inwards as if about to fall in and crush him.

One four-storey tenement block had cardboard railings fronting it. Stave could see undefined shapes moving beyond the cardboard window frames. He was transfixed awhile until he tore his sight away to glance up to a direction sign on a cardboard post. It read, "To the Square". Stave turned in the direction of the arrow, and once through a forbidding and shadowy cardboard alley, came out into the grey light of the municipal square.

33 : DISCOVERING THE LOST CUTOUTS

BROWN CARDBOARD SHOPS with cardboard offices above, cardboard kiosks and larger buildings, dominated each side of the square. In the centre stood a sizeable cardboard fountain, the water in its base turned to grey sludge. Cardboard street lamps were about it, casting a blue light.

There were scores of cardboard cutouts of people standing across the square, with crude grey paint for faces and clothes. Some of those cutouts, still articulated at the joints, twitched or flinched as though attempting movement. Others stood, flat, around cardboard steps leading to a plinth. A cardboard statue stood upon the plinth, disfigured with grey paint. A few of the cutouts were attempting to fold themselves into cardboard boxes. Others tried to speak, weird utterances coming from their downturned, painted mouths of 'te-te-te', 'mm-mm-mm' and 'zz-zz-zz'. Their mumbles together sounded like a nest of flies or a hive of bees.

Stave bowed his head with sorrow. These were captured spirits, sucked of life. Emptied souls, those which had been as clear as cut glass, now dulled, shattered and defiled. Beings seemingly beyond help or rescue.

Once a fine town with fine people…

On one side of the square stood a tall building, and had it been made of granite blocks, would have been imposing. Nonetheless, even made of cardboard, with its high, fluted columns and massive double doors, it was impressive.

Above the columns, scrawled in untidy grey paint, were the words "Public Library". Directly opposite, on the other side of the heart-strewn and cardboard cutout-populated square, stood an identical building, except its words, painted as though in haste on the cardboard beam on top of the pillars, read "Town Hall".

Behind, towering above the grim cardboard town, stood a plain-sided grey box – a warehouse, magnificently huge, as tall as a mountain, wreathed with dark grey clouds at its squared-off summit. Blue smoke emitted from its many open windows. The whole of the massive warehouse, forbidding and eerie, quivered and shook now and then as though shivering with cold. Grating, scraping and deep rasping noises from it moved down the lonely cardboard streets as if made by an invisible beast in search of prey.

Stave felt a load upon him, as though a mighty weight had been placed over his head and shoulders. He must escape its oppressive presence: he ran up the cardboard steps of the library and pushed on one of the cardboard doors.

34 : RECEPTION TO THE NIGHTMARE

HE ENTERED INTO an oval reception hall, high and wide, with grand pillars which once had been chiselled marble, and panels on the curving wall. They had all been turned into mottled cardboard. A grey and blue coral-like crust spread over some of the walls like a diseased rash.

He went up to the cardboard reception desk, a lamp on it projecting a grey pool of light. An agent of Tremelon stood behind the desk. His funereal mask was like that of a young woman with eyes closed, even mouth, and nostrils dilated. Stave was unsure whether or not to trust this abominable person; he walked furtively up to him.

'Table. Not. For. One,' the agent stated in a strangled female voice.

'Don't take your mask off to open your despicable eyes then I'll talk to you,' Stave said. His voice echoed strangely. The agent merely nodded. Stave continued, 'Where is Tremelon Zandar?'

'You. Won't. Know,' the agent said, the eyes on his mask opening slightly before closing again.

'I know? So my hunch is correct; I'm getting nearer.'

The agent's guttural, animal-like reply: 'You'll. Find. Him.

He'll. Never. Find. You.'

'I'll never find him, he'll find me – well, we'll see.'

Do we tremble at repellant sights, a turning from them being the only purging? At those words, the agent partly removed his mask by pulling down with a clawed hand, to expose the eyes underneath. Those deep-set eyes flicked open. Metal serpents' heads looked out from the eye sockets, with their forked tongues flickering.

Stave's head and sight whipped away but this was no purgative, the image still fresh in its grim form. He felt an oppressive, ugly pain with energy drawn from his third eye, heart, and solar plexus. He clamped his teeth tightly, his limbs losing strength. The coral-like encrustations about him on the walls gained density, each floret multiplying, filaments of blue spawning at a fast rate and sparking like incarnadine fireflies. The cardboard tiles on the floor began to undulate and Stave felt as sick as if on a rough sea journey. The agent of Tremelon began to remove the rest of the mask and dread gripped Stave's mind as tightly as if a vice were squeezing his brain.

My head hurting so much. Please be correct, Cassaldra, let dream logic be simple…

In slow-motion, the movement painfully difficult to manage, he moved his right hand to the inside pocket of his jacket, taking hold of the mirror and the magnifying glass. He enlarged the mirror while blue smoke emitted out of the metallic serpents' jaws coming from the agent's eyes. Stave, still gripped with horror and depletion of energy, lifted the mirror up with the last of his strength.

Instantly, with a backwards hacking cough of a sound, the

serpents retracted to leave empty eye sockets. The agent hurriedly placed back the mask, the face upon it now that of an old man, fine wrinkles about the relaxed mouth and on the forehead, eyelids closed in peaceful rest.

'Don't. Go. Through,' the agent said in a guttural voice.

'I shall then,' Stave answered, recovering his composure. He reduced the mirror in size before putting in back into a pocket. Then he walked across the cardboard floor tiles to the side of the desk, out of the grey spotlight, over to another set of cardboard double doors, and pushed.

35 : KNOWLEDGE TURNED TO CARDBOARD

HE CAME INTO an inner lobby. A cardboard screen ahead of him, reaching from ceiling to floor, made the fourth wall.

Impressive statues were set in alcoves, both at least fifteen feet height. On the left side, the imposing statue of a man stood, his cloak made of cardboard. And on the right, a carefully rendered sculpture of a woman sat in repose, wearing a cardboard gown. The man pointed to his head while the woman pointed to her heart. Both were defaced with graffiti scrawled in grey paint.

What entrapment now? What talents needed to escape the conspiring confines of another bad dream, the lobby seemingly innocuous but foreboding all the same? Deeper into the mind of Tremelon as a prisoner, energies depleting.

The statues either side of him burst into flames.

Stave pushed the cardboard wall as a way of escape but it felt as solid as if made of bricks and mortar. He turned around again but the door through which he had entered from the reception hall had vanished. In its place, an oil painting hung, showing the cottage with the stark landscape as its background.

He heard a babble of voices coming from the cardboard

screen. They rose to a crescendo of gabbling, then to whispers, and back again to full volume. Interspersing this was orchestra music playing in balanced unison, only to degenerate into a raucous row as if they were all tuning their instruments at the same time, before slowly evolving to melodic music again. The whole creating a sea of sounds, waves of them ebbing and flowing in loudness and quality.

The cardboard screen split into two and opened slightly.

'Welcome! We are the true oasis in the desert, the refuge from the storm. I'll be your head waiter,' said a man from the interior who had wheeled up to him on a skateboard.

Welcome to more confusion, you mean.

'Your eyes. What's happened to them?' Stave asked, taken aback.

The man had empty sockets where eyes used to be.

'What do you mean, sir? I can see perfectly well. Grey and the blue. Vivid, blood red soon. I'm noticing your aura is dimming – excellent, you are giving up, sir. Good man, bad man, sir.'

Stave caught sight of the interior behind him, consisting of rows of high bookcases filled with brown books, balconies above with the same.

'Let me show you to your dream table,' the head waiter continued, 'before you burn to death. That's not the death we want now, is it? We want a proper death. Full à la carte, will it be? We have coppered fish steaks in battered wine curds, simple beef custard with semolina tartlets, to name a few. The speciality of the day is liver cakelets in meringue sauce. Especially delicious at celebration time.' He gave a pleasant, broad smile before handing Stave a menu. 'You'll find the wine list on your table, sir. We have all rarities – finely strained, minuet and mortified amongst others. Choose to your delight. A fine suit you are wearing, I must say. Turquoise, isn't it, so I've been told. That's my favourite colour. Interesting choice. We've been expecting you. Your last ever meal, sir?'

'I'm not certain I understand you. Is this your dream or one given you by Tremelon Zandar?'

'No, no, surely, sirness, this is yours. Have you bought your book?'

'My book? What book?' Stave replied. 'Please hurry, this fire is getting hotter.'

'You've come to the public library dinner service without your book? Tut, tut, sir. We'll have to check your validity here.' Then there was the ticking of a clock and the sound of the head waiter's breathing in and out. He distorted his lips to a vaguely absurd expression, his eyebrows raising and lowering in time to the timepiece. 'One moment please, while I check with the management who checks the management.'

He skated away through the gap in the cardboard screen.

Stave followed, away from the heat of the burning statues, into the large hall with balconies and bookcases.

As the gentle tinkering of a piano emanated throughout the library, the bookcases creaked, sounding as if from some wooden sea vessel in a gale.

36 : FEASTERS OF THE DREAM

ALONG EACH AISLE of bookcases at floor level, as well as the three balconies, stood rows of tables with turquoise tablecloths over them. Upon each table were cardboard plates and cutlery, and a candelabra holding candles that gave out a greyish light. Diners sat, dressed in their finest clothes, up to ten per table. As Stave entered, they immediately ceased their loud and excited conversations. All turned their heads to him and stood, then clapped their hands enthusiastically. Even the waiters on skateboards, holding lidded trays, came to a standstill and patted their thighs, adding to the applause that began to set up a regular rhythm of its own.

The cowbells about the diners' necks rattled all at once. An agent of Tremelon stood at the end of each aisle, and they spoke at the same time.

'Not. Welcome. To. Your. Heaven. Don't. Dine. And. Live.'

Now, imagined chinking from wine glasses made of cardboard by the guests.

The constant rhythmic clapping began to echo in Stave's head, pounding like a headache. The applause was insistent. On it went, that clapped rhythm, becoming more painful by the second.

Please stop.

He took the tiny metronome from a pocket of his turquoise suit pocket and enlarged it to proper size using the magnifying glass. He set the speed to the beat of the claps then stopped it to adjust the speed to slow before started the metronome again. The clapping slowed to match it. He repeated the process, setting the metronome beat even slower until there was silence from them, other than the occasional single clap, murmur or self-conscious laugh.

Each one of the innocent diners were in their own bubble of existence. One of them sensed he was feasting in the luxury carriage of a railway train, another on board a romantic yacht, yet another in a palatial palace. They were being fed cardboard. This they did not see: what they saw was fine cuisine, exquisite culinary formulations, and ultimate sensations on the tongue – superlative tastes with wondrous delight to their stomachs.

The laughter and happy conversations from those on the library floors increased; the hidden orchestra played discordant notes again.

Their souls being stolen by Tremelon Zandar, I see. They are easily manipulated before being turned into nothing more than cardboard. This place is to judge their reactions and resilience to nightmare. At the moment, they are in a wonderful lucid dream that they believe is their reward. Little do they know what's in store for them.

Wake up, he wanted to shout but knew it would be of no use. The diners were too deeply within their dream world that would be turning to nightmare.

I have to carry on the journey, somehow. I need to save Cassaldra. And stop more souls from being stolen. Have to get out of here.

'It. Is. Not. Time,' all the agents at the ends of the table said at once.

Stave experienced a magnetic energy coming from under the first balcony, as strong as that he had experienced from the horse skeleton. This time though, he managed to stagger backwards into the lobby, resisting it. As he did so, the ground floor and the balconies of the library descended without sound, as if the library was a massive lift. That left a cavernous, dark space within a massive structure, the corners of it far above, lost in deep shadow.

He advanced unwillingly into the morbid and echoing warehouse.

37 : WAREHOUSE OF WRITHING PIPES

HE CAME UPON a steam engine on its side, with the carriages upside down. They were scattered across the vast, grey area as if they had been swept away by a giant hand. Hiding inside them were more people who had been turned into cardboard cutouts. They peered out of the grimy windows, giving their utterances of 'te-te-te', 'mm-mm-mm' and 'zz-zz-zz'.

Stave made his way between the hefty carriages with their wheels in the air, to tangles of grey pipes on the featureless floor.

The further into the warehouse he ventured, the more pipes he could see, each side of him. Their ends twisted and turned, rattled, and spurted blue steam.

A foreboding, an inkling of what was to come: Stave's skin itched as though covered with insects. A distinct malevolence in the air.

Lost in nothing but evil – I sense that.

Shipping containers, painted in blue and nine feet high, barred his way. On top of them were mannequins who looked down at him with unblinking stares. Still they glowed as if lit by neon. Stave found a gap between two of the containers, walking between them with his head up, suspiciously eyeing the mannequins in return. They followed his progress from their vantage point. There was an aisle at the end of the gap. Another line of containers ran the length of it. Some of the animated dummies leapt over that gap onto the top of one of them.

Stave turned into the aisle and walked the length of it to the last container in the row. He walked around it and the mannequins seemed to lose interest in him.

Ahead, surrounded by scattered cardboard boxes and writhing inner tubes, stood a mass of articulated pipes – fifty feet across or more, the colour of dark turquoise. They vibrated as they vigorously moved. They curved and curled around each other, disappearing and re-emerging, slithering like huge metallic worms, always in continuous motion.

Through stinging eyes, Stave watched the intertwining pipes rise quickly above the floor. Below the pipes a massive mask was exposed, at least thirty feet high, eyes closed on the pale and waxen visage. He recognised it as his own face. The mask continued to rise, then he could see the squirming pipes completely surrounded the death mask, Medusa-like.

Stave gasped at the extraordinary sight ahead of him.

Finally, I meet my adversary – the evil Tremelon Zandar, hiding behind a mask resembling my features.

To his left stood an audience: more agents of Tremelon. Their faces were as pale death masks, placid, with eyes closed. Like the mannequins on top of the containers, they appeared disinterested in him, satisfied only to stand and watch.

They spoke in unison.

'You. Don't. Belong. To. Us.'

The towering, massive mask hovered in the air. Deep

growling came from it as if the amplified sounds from a vicious animal.

All about Stave dimmed except for the mask. At the periphery of his vision were strange dart-shaped turrets, and spiked shapes illuminated in purple. Before him, Cassaldra as her elderly version stood in a large, grey teapot up to her waist. The skin on her face and arms was crimson red.

'Help me, Stave, I'm burning, I'm burning,' she cried and gave anguished screams. As she spoke, chicken bones came from out of her mouth. They fell to the floor and lay there, twitching. Stave's heart lurched.

He ran towards the teapot and took hold of Cassaldra under her arms, ready to haul her out. But she transformed into a side of bacon. The mottled red and white flesh felt slippery and cold. More screams came from it. Was this really Cassaldra being tortured, or just a nightmare?

Either way, Stave recoiled from it, a feeling of revulsion overtaking him. He turned and almost tripped over an open coffin. Inside lay the side of bacon, with crabs scuttling over its surface.

He couldn't tear his sight away as the glistening flesh rose and fell as if breathing. He looked up as he recognised the voice of someone who spoke.

'She was a good woman.' It was Quickso Lebum. Stave looked back to the open coffin and saw that Mariella lay there on her back, pulling legs from some of the live crabs.

Quikso, with his tongue poking in and out, looked to Stave before reaching out and grabbing him by the throat.

'Give up,' the nightmare of Quikso said.

Stave held onto the wrists, attempting to pull his hands

away. He felt his windpipe being crushed as he gasped for air. Quikso's face changed; it was now Cassaldra holding him. She let go.

'Prepare your soul for evacuation,' she said as her mouth widened and turned downwards in an ugly fashion.

Stave panted hoarsely and massaged his sore neck.

'You're not Cassaldra; leave me be,' he managed to say. 'I realise you are trying to turn my mind, to lead me into madness, but it's not going to work.'

With that said, Stave saw the pipes around the giant mask emitting metal serpent heads from their ends. The serpents let out blue smoke from their jaws while more came from the floor. Nausea and fright enveloped him.

The blue smoke quickly thickened and drifted over to him. Stave was choking from it, his lungs filling with the noxious gases. Condemned to suffocation, he coughed as though his lungs might burst, clutching a hand to his mouth and nose.

This is the end. Windpipe being ripped from me, my very essence leaching away as those demonic metallic snakes give out their foul stench.

While the odorous fog of blue smoke billowed in the air, shouts of anger, screams and cries of help came from within the moving, larger pipes.

Stave staggered back across the hot floor, through the smoke billows, struggling to breathe within the toxic fumes.

He must get out before the gas overpowered him. Already he felt sick and giddy, his lungs hurting badly. He clutched at his stinging throat and still coughed hoarsely.

Life being ripped from from my body. My only hope is dream logic to save me.

Searching hurriedly in an inside pocket of his jacket he found his small brown bottle of cough mixture. He took it out, quickly unscrewed the cap, and drank greedily from it. He gasped for air in between draughts. At first there was no change but after the third or fourth gulp of liquid, he felt his windpipe clearing and the taste of menthol in his mouth. Eventually the cough mixture completely eased his aching lungs and shortened breath. The clouds of blue smoke began to disperse.

Even though I know it would be the end if the mask was removed, I'm almost intrigued by what he really looks like behind it. Serpents coming out of empty eye sockets like his agents? Multiple layers of teeth? Upside-down mouth grinning like the demon he surely is?

Without warning, the enormous mask began to dissolve, the pipes and snakes about it becoming even more energetic.

Stave felt his limbs losing energy, a pulling sensation as though by some organic magnet again, towards the massive face underneath the mask. He daren't look at it, already feeling his very soul ripping from him.

Haunted by demonic thoughts taking over, his mind unravelling...

He was succumbing, the final nightmare enveloping him. He sank to his knees, resigned to his fate, holding his head as it pounded as painfully as if from hammer blows, lost in that shroud of evil.

Articulated cardboard cutouts came jerking and jolting from out of the darkness. They advanced upon Stave with determination, giving their monosyllabic utterances, joining cardboard hands and making a line of defence between him and Tremelon Zandar.

They were protecting him from seeing his true face. Stave was grateful. He must act fast to save himself – and save all others in the dream realm, including those cardboard cutouts who once were people.

A few moments to think through his next course of action. He must still follow logic, the rules of the dream.

'To defeat Tremelon is simple,' he repeated to himself.

He decided what he must do: he retrieved both the mirror and the magnifying glass from his pocket. With his back turned on the cardboard cutouts and Tremelon Zandar, made the mirror larger with the aid of the magnifying glass, like he had done in the library foyer. Then he held up the mirror as high as he could manage, judging where best to capture the reflection of the evil face. With the other hand, he held up the magnifying glass, holding it the opposite way of enlargement, and placing it in front of the mirror.

For a moment, nothing happening of consequence until there were deep howlings and booms like thunder, and vociferous roars like that from an erupting volcano. Stave dared to turn back around, gently pushing through the line of protective cutouts. And there before him, the serpents were no bigger than small worms about the normal-sized head of Tremelon Zandar on grey metal plates of the warehouse floor.

Stave caught a glimpse of the hideous face and it felt as if someone had pushed a knife into his brain. It was indescribable and haunted his vision, seeing it whichever way he turned. He reeled from the pain of it but continued on his mission. He ran to an empty cardboard box and picked it up. He daren't take a chance of seeing the true face again so he walked backwards. And once near enough to the head with its writhing pipes and serpents, quickly placed the box over it.

He turned around, and continued to reduce the box and its hideous contents in size using the magnifying glass, only stopping when it was beyond a mere speck.

Immediately his body became energised as dissipation of his life forces ceased, and he was no longer under control of the evil and cunning Tremelon Zandar.

Explosions of colour like paint tins exploding, a beautiful melody haunting the smokeless atmosphere? Neither of these happenings, just a relieved air of finality in the warehouse and of peace at last, no sounds to upset a deep silence.

The cardboard cutouts had vanished. The agents of Tremelon had taken their masks off and were rubbing their returned eyes as if they had come out of deep sleep, appearing confused and lost. They began losing definition, fading away from the dream realm, back to everyday reality.

Stave walked further on through the warehouse, now neatly stacked with empty cardboard boxes, and scaffolding holding up water towers. He was alert and feeling more awake than he had for a long time.

In the not so far distance ahead, he saw a square of light: an exit.

38 : BEGINNING OF ETERNITY ANEW

STAVE CAME OUT into a sunlit glade with a clean and fresh atmosphere, the sounds of a waterfall from afar. He looked behind him. In place of the warehouse was a verdant mountain. It was pleasantly warm as he made his way across immaculate grass, accompanied by a light scented breeze and bird song from amongst the trees.

Cassaldra Chimewood appeared from out of strong light shafts, rays of light emanating from her. She was dressed in a long gown patterned with silk, her hair plaited, her young and attractive features alive, her eyes bright as she smiled.

'You have defeated Tremelon Zandar. Welcome home.'

A shower of rose petals fell from the fragrant air.

A glimmer of more recognition. I am in love with this young woman, I'm beginning to believe it.

'You can hug me if you want,' Cassaldra said.

Stave held her close, her perfume enveloping him. It felt natural and right.

'I have hints that I've loved you for a long time but yet still can't recall,' Stave said as they parted and held hands.

Cassaldra lowered her head, her plaited hair falling over her characterful face, hiding sadness there, that same sadness washing through Stave's mind.

'I'll learn to love you again,' he said.

They strolled through the glade, surrounded by enormous handsome trees, and Cassaldra replied, 'I know. Now the agents of Tremelon have been vanquished as well, you will begin to remember again and never forget. I will explain everything – I will teach you.'

'Thank you. Who was Tremelon Zandar?'

'Maybe fragments of all of our personalities,' said Cassaldra. 'Perhaps he was what mortals call a fallen angel. Perhaps it was a test by a higher agency. Or part of your unconscious mind magnified, for you to resolve: the dream within your own realm becoming a nightmare, a puzzle for you to solve. Whoever or whatever he was, he is no longer here, now that he has been eradicated. And maybe your journey has been a lesson, part of another spiritual mountain to climb – the understanding of your next level of reality. But first, you have to be taught all that you knew before, in this reality. This is your realm, your own personal heaven, now united and repaired.'

'I'm not fully understanding what you're telling me.'

'Soon you will,' Cassaldra answered as they passed a lake, alive with orange and yellow coy carp. 'Let me start by mentioning that through all your lives, you have never harmed another being.'

'All my lives?'

'You have lived in previous lives, Stave, as well as the one you're living in now. All of us here have. It is the learning process of true life. And you attained an understanding of the next level of reality. Because of that, you deserved and was given your own reality, do you see? Let us discuss more when we've reached the cottage.'

'But the cottage was destroyed...'

'What you saw was Tremelon Zandar's evil interpretation of the cottage, what he wanted you to believe had really happened. This is all real and whole again now.'

'Yes, I haven't felt so real in a long while.'

They reached a rose-entwined arch to the cottage garden that was plentiful with blooms and wildflowers. In one corner stood an elegant summerhouse next to moss-covered boulders.

'There, let us rest,' Cassaldra said.

They sat inside with warm shadows over them, silent for a while, just looking at each other.

'Please be patient with me as I try to understand all of this,' Stave said finally.

'Of course, I have patience. We can always visit here again at this same day and time for you to remember even more.'

'Doesn't that make a mockery of time?'

'Time here in this realm can be as meaningful as you want it to be.'

'What does that even mean?' Stave said.

'No matter for the while,' Cassaldra replied. 'Let us leave time manipulation for another day. First though, you must practice dream summoning in your reality.'

'I've had some experience of that with limited success as you know.'

'One day you will be even better, as proficient as you were before the forgetting. Orange juice with ice and lemon?'

Stave laughed.

'As it happens, I would like one of those.' Two filled glasses appeared on a table beside them. 'Did I summon them or did you?'

'A bit of both,' Cassaldra answered. 'Soon you'll be strong enough to dream summon anything at any time without too much effort.' A becoming smile lit her face. Stave looked to her, this young woman emanating pure love. She continued, 'Dream summoning is a powerful resource here in our realm. Anything of positive good for yourself or for others is possible. Maybe you would like to open a portal to a tea plantation or arrange a visit to a dream cast travel agent beforehand. Or decide you want to meet others for a social event. Then by walking out of your cottage and down the lane you'll find what was previously not there. Perhaps a tavern filled with noisy and happy folk – your friends, imagined and real. Whatever you wish for becomes reality, as magical or as ordinary as you like. You can have your positive dreams made real. We are creative artists of the dream reality.'

'Where is this dream reality?'

'In our minds, and our minds are all around us. We are pure thought, spirit, love, and energy. We can create anything from the normal to the magnificent: fly in metal birds between cloud stations, create adventure games, stroll across bronze and marble walkways high up in sapphire cities. Or if you wish to be particularly creative, imagine fish racing over fragrant landscapes, or air swimming through the land of the tiny creatures. Imagine other dreams within reality – investigate active volcanos, walking over its rivers of molten lava, for instance. Eventually create mountains and valleys, plains, cities, jungles and wildernesses. Beyond the forest lies many incredible places, already built by combined mental energies. Do you see? Anything is possible; anything you wish for can become.'

'That's all too much for me to take in at the moment. I still have many questions though,' Stave said.

'Yes, sorry, too much too soon. As to your questions, some can be answered, others will be shown, but all in your own time.'

'What about failure? Unless that's part of the process of self-discovery?'

'You have learned that already, Stave,' Cassaldra said. 'Any obstacle can be put into your own path if that's your wish. Positive random dream sculpting you will be taught again, as well as time manipulation.'

'Isn't it hard work?'

'Sometimes, but isn't all creativity? You will be helped by many, including myself, and by the keepers of the chasm.'

'Yes, I've met those. Who are they?'

Cassaldra shook her head.

'No one knows for certain; they are mysterious beings. But for sure, they have their own realm beyond even our imaginings.'

'And what about Mariella Fortana and Quikso Lebum, for instance?' Stave picked up his glass of orange juice from the table and sipped it.

Beyond the beautiful garden, a small herd of redback deer stood, eating grass stems by a lake of orchids.

Cassaldra answered, 'They are adventurers, like yourself, who were invited to your realm. They too have earned their own realms. You will see them again. They'll join you many times for real dream adventures where you'll meet other adventure players. Some are part of your own personality, others are gods and goddesses, and more invited from the mortal realm. And within those games, you can be anyone you wish. Already you are known by many epithets: keeper of the keys, purveyor of wondrous journeys, dream master, to name some.'

'You mentioned gods and goddesses?'

Cassaldra still glowed with an aura of light.

'Like we are. You are a god, Stave Swirler; I am a goddess. We are ancient, immortal. We can no longer die unless we choose to. You invited me to your heaven many years ago and I can invite you to mine. Part of my heaven is to revisit past lives, not as an observer but to relive them as many times as I wish. We have known each other for centuries. Now we have another joyous mountain to climb, spiritually speaking, but this time without pain, hurt, greed or anger. Learn to live and love again, learn to be free. We have many wonders ahead of us, and to know we will never suffer physically or mentally again.'

The only tears are tears of happiness. Someone told me that a long time ago...

That thought triggered a rush of memory. Stave's heart lurched with love as he gazed at Cassaldra, fully recognising her.

'I'm remembering again!' he cried out, and he knelt before her, took her delicate hand and kissed it. 'My Cassaldra,' he said.

'Stave,' she answered simply and stroked his hair.

I will love you again forever with every atom of my being. You are my dream reality.

A clear crystalline space, a pause encompassing spirit and soul.

Beyond the passage of time, outside of pain and death, a god and goddess kissed as two halves of the same entity. A simple kiss of empathy, love, and unity within a sphere of silvery light. And for an eternity of joy within a fleeting moment, they became one.

If you enjoyed reading Turquoise Traveller please consider leaving a review on Amazon – thank you.

Turquoise Traveller is also available as a Kindle ebook.

David John Griffin is a writer, graphic designer and app designer, and lives in a small town by the Thames in Kent, UK with his wife Susan and two dogs called Bullseye and Jimbo. He is currently working on the final draft of a fifth novel.

His first novel, *The Unusual Possession of Alastair Stubb*, was published by Urbane Publishing in November 2015. Urbane also published David's literary/psychological novel entitled *Infinite Rooms*, as well as his magical realism/paranormal novella, *Two Dogs At The One Dog Inn And Other Stories*. His fourth book called *Abbie and the Portal* (a science fiction time travel adventure) was published in 2018. One of his short stories was shortlisted for The HG Wells Short Story competition in 2012 and published in an anthology. He has several other stories published in various collections.

You can find out more about David at
www.davidjohngriffin.com

Also available on Amazon:

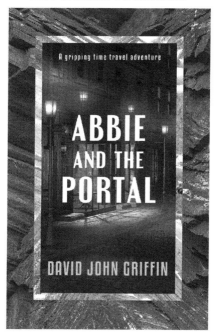

ABBIE AND THE PORTAL

"Help me, I'm trapped" is the plea from a young woman
named Abbie Concordia, written as a mysterious note
found inside a Victorian book called Caving in
Faringham. Terry Bridge, a reporter for The Charington
Echo, takes up the challenge to save her...from the past.
A gripping sci-fi time travel adventure story that will
captivate you from beginning to end.

"Great premise, scintillating pace, and a most
intriguing plot"
"Utterly absorbing"
"A story that had me engrossed from the start"

43633182R00130

Printed in Poland
by Amazon Fulfillment
Poland Sp. z o.o., Wrocław